BIG MATCH MANAGER

EUROPEAN CUP FOOTBALL

BIG MATCH MANAGER
TOM SHELDON

EUROPEAN CUP FOOTBALL

ILLUSTRATED BY
NATHAN BURTON

BLOOMSBURY
CHILDREN'S
BOOKS

For Joe and Eliza

First published in Great Britain in 2006 by Bloomsbury Publishing Plc
36 Soho Square, London, W1D 3QY

Text copyright © 2006 by Tom Sheldon
Illustrations copyright © 2006 by Nathan Burton
The moral rights of the author and illustrator have been asserted

All rights reserved. No part of this publication may be reproduced or
transmitted by any means, electronic, mechanical, photocopying
or otherwise, without the prior permission of the publisher

A CIP catalogue record of this book is available from the British Library

ISBN 0 7475 8205 X
9780747582052

All papers used by Bloomsbury Publishing are natural, recyclable products made from wood
grown in well-managed forests. The manufacturing processes conform to the environmental
regulations of the country of origin.

Printed in Great Britain by Clays Ltd, St Ives Plc

1 3 5 7 9 10 8 6 4 2

www.bigmatchmanager.com
www.bloomsbury.com/childrens

Getting Started

This is a book with a difference. You don't open it at page one and keep reading until the end like any other book. Instead, YOU play the central character – and by making decisions as you go along, you change what happens! In this book, every paragraph has a number. At the end of each paragraph, you may be asked to make a choice – and you will be told which paragraph number to turn to. If you haven't read this kind of book before, don't worry – it's easy once you get started. But you will need some basic items before you begin: a pencil, an eraser, and a pair of six-sided dice. (If you can't find any dice, you'll notice that at the bottom of every page a pair of dice has been printed for you. When you are told to roll dice, just close the book and open it at a random page – and there's your dice roll for you.)

In this story you are the manager of Hardwick City Football Club, and under your guidance the team stands on the brink of European footballing glory. You steered them to the top of the table last season, and your prize is a place in the most prestigious footballing competition in Europe. As you progress through the book you will play against some of the best teams on the continent; but things aren't as simple as they seem. More about that later.

The Fact Sheet

Even the best managers can't remember everything, so on page 282 at the back of the book you have been provided with a **Fact**

Sheet. This is where you write down all your team information and match results, as well as the clues and objects you collect as you go along. But remember to always use a pencil so you can rub things out if they change, or if you play the book all over again. Remember you can be the Big Match Manager as many times as you like!

You start the season with a **Budget** of 10 million pounds at your disposal. This is so you can buy new players as you go along. Write it in the space at the top of your Fact Sheet now. Ten million doesn't go far these days, and sometimes you might decide you want to sell a player to another club to bump up your bank account. You'll be told which players can be bought and sold as you go along. But you may never let your Budget slip below zero. It's in your contract!

Next on the Fact Sheet you'll see your **Fixture List**. This tells you which other teams are in the league with you, and what order you'll be playing them in.

After that come your team's **Morale** and **Fitness**.

Morale describes the general mood of your team. Winning matches and good management help improve morale. Roll 1 dice. (If you're using the dice printed in this book, just use the one on the left.) This number is the Morale you start the book with – you can write it on your Fact Sheet now. Morale will change as you make your way through this book.

Fitness is a measure of how well trained your squad is. Fit and healthy players can run faster on the pitch and recover from injuries more quickly. Roll 1 dice again – this is the Fitness you start with. Write it on the Fact Sheet. Like Morale, your Fitness level will change as the book goes on.

Your Team

At the end of the Fact Sheet you'll see your **Squad Details**. You have eighteen players in your Squad to choose from, and it's up to you to select your best team before each match is played. No two players are alike, and each of them has a different **Skill**. This is a single number which reflects everything about that player's footballing ability: the higher the better. They've all got different personalities, strengths and weaknesses; and certain combinations of footballers play well together. So read on: it's time to get to know your team.

Player Profiles

Jamie Coates

Skill:	5		Last Season's Stats:	
Position:	Goalkeeper		Goals:	0
Born:	Fife 2/9/70		Yellow Cards:	1
Height:	6ft 3in		Red Cards:	0
Weight:	13st 0lb			

Rock solid goal-mouth performances year after year from Coates have secured him the No. 1 shirt in your team, and after Knox he is your second choice captain too. Jamie still has the stickiest fingers in the business, and last season he broke all league records for number of clean sheets. But with maturity comes age, and Jamie is no spring chicken. He knows he has to keep

JAMIE COATES

turning out match-saving performances to keep you happy.

Rob Rose

Skill:	5		Last Season's Stats:	
Position:	Goalkeeper		Goals:	0
Born:	Oxford 31/12/81		Yellow Cards:	0
Height:	6ft 1in		Red Cards:	0
Weight:	12st 9lb			

Close behind comes Rob Rose, and at eleven years Coates' junior he feels it's only a matter of time before the regular spot is his. He's been patiently working at his game the past few years, and his youthful hot-headedness has been replaced by a determined aptitude for keeping goal. Hardwick's biggest emerging talent?

ROB ROSE

Steve Fitzgerald

Skill:	5	Last Season's Stats:	
Position:	Defender	Goals:	0
Born:	Liverpool 19/9/78	Yellow Cards:	3
Height:	6ft 1in	Red Cards:	2
Weight:	10st 7lb		

Pairs well with: de Carvalho (D), Bostock (M)

From one season to the next, this full-back never changes. Quiet and private off the pitch, sometimes it's easy to forget he's there; but when he was out for six weeks last winter with a fractured metatarsal, the whole team noticed his absence. This stalwart forms the backbone of your defence, and has the physical capabilities to cope with everything the modern game can throw at him.

STEVE FITZGERALD

Howie Jevons

Skill: 5
Position: Defender
Born: Brighton 30/12/86
Height: 5ft 11in
Weight: 12st 2lb

Last Season's Stats:
Goals: 0
Yellow Cards: 4
Red Cards: 0

Pairs well with: Roberts (M)

The hallmark of any great player is time and space on the ball: this young back stick has both. When you first saw him in a local U16 match he played the others off the park, and you immediately signed him to your own youth academy where his talent continues to grow. Sure-footed, swift and with a self-confidence that belies his age.

HOWIE JEVONS

Antek Bobak

Skill: 5
Position: Defender
Born: Krakow 17/6/75
Height: 5ft 11in
Weight: 11st 9lb

Last Season's Stats:
Goals: 1
Yellow Cards: 2
Red Cards: 2

Pairs well with: Voss (D)

Equally at home at left-back or in a sweeper's role, this Pole is a real live wire and can be unpredictable on the pitch. He's a bit of a rebel, a maverick who doesn't play by the rules. But he's the complete package: cool as a cucumber at the back, and capable of visionary passes up-field to create goal-scoring chances from apparently nothing.

ANTEK BOBAK

Barry Voss

		Last Season's Stats:	
Skill:	5		
Position:	Defender	Goals:	0
Born:	London 16/2/84	Yellow Cards:	4
Height:	6ft 0in	Red Cards:	0
Weight:	13st 4lb		

Pairs well with: Bobak (D), Frost (M)

'He's not the best, but there are none better.' That's how Voss was once famously described in a newspaper report, and you've always wondered what the reporter meant. Certainly, when he decides to play to his ability, he can guard the box like it's welded shut. But at other times he can be prone to schoolboy errors. Needs the guiding hand of a confident manager.

BARRY VOSS

Carlos de Carvalho

Skill:	6		Last Season's Stats:	
Position:	Defender		Goals:	0
Born:	Lisbon 5/8/82		Yellow Cards:	3
Height:	6ft 1in		Red Cards:	1
Weight:	11st 1lb			

Pairs well with: Fitzgerald (D), Duval (M)

Ever the showman, Carlos's flair on the ball is matched only by his bling off it. He reportedly makes more now as a pin-up than as a footballer, and you recently had to put a rocket up him when he tried to get out of training because he was doing a photo shoot for *Vogue*. But however many beautiful women he's seen with, he never loses his passion for the beautiful game. A living defensive legend.

CARLOS DE CARVALHO

Will 'Frog' Frost

Skill:	5		Last Season's Stats:	
Position:	Midfielder		Goals:	2
Born:	Birmingham 15/4/75		Yellow Cards:	2
Height:	5ft 9in		Red Cards:	1
Weight:	10st 10lb			

Pairs well with: Duce (A)

One of Hardwick's elder statesmen, Frost has established himself as your regular No. 8 shirt. The rest of the squad looks to him to produce momentum in the midfield, and his intelligent, tactical play allows you to throw men forward in sudden, lethal counter-attacks. Unselfish passing and an assured finish when it counts make Frost a dangerous attacking midfielder.

WILL 'FROG' FROST

Zaki Roberts

Skill: 6
Position: Midfielder
Born: London 7/6/88
Height: 6ft 0in
Weight: 11st 8lb

Last Season's Stats:
Goals: 6
Yellow Cards: 3
Red Cards: 1

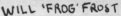

Pairs well with: Jevons (D), Wehnert (M)

This guy's got an engine on him. A new addition to your squad, Zaki is a very talented youngster, and he has the lungs and legs to prove it: no other midfielder will beat him for pace up front. This lad moves so fast, one day he'll start heading in his own crosses.

ZAKI ROBERTS

Anthony 'Asbo' Bostock

Skill:	5	Last Season's Stats:	
Position:	Midfielder	Goals:	2
Born:	Brighton 28/3/80	Yellow Cards:	2
Height:	6ft 0in	Red Cards:	0
Weight:	11st 8lb		

Pairs well with: Fitzgerald (D), Stevens (A)

Still the master of the dead-ball: six of Hardwick's fifteen goals so far in the European qualifiers have come off an Asbo corner or free kick. Still the master of the wind-up as well: he played so many practical jokes on the team last season you threatened him with a new nickname. It stuck.

ANTHONY BOSTOCK

Klaus 'The General' Wehnert

Skill:	6	Last Season's Stats:	
Position:	Midfielder	Goals:	3
Born:	Stuttgart 18/11/76	Yellow Cards:	0
Height:	6ft 4in	Red Cards:	1
Weight:	13st 12lb		

Pairs well with: Roberts (M), Leslie (A)

You know the kind of player who is so reliable, everyone breathes a sigh of relief when he gets the ball? Klaus is one of them. He can mow down opposition midfielders while rarely losing possession or committing a foul. The sheer size of this centre, together with his extraordinary deftness of touch, means he can put the ball exactly where he wants it and tackles just bounce off him.

KLAUS 'THE GENERAL' WEHNERT

John 'Larry' Hoggart

		Last Season's Stats:	
Skill:	5		
Position:	Midfielder	Goals:	1
Born:	Tasmania 1/7/79	Yellow Cards:	2
Height:	6ft 1in	Red Cards:	1
Weight:	11st 9lb		

Pairs well with: Parker (A), Knox (A)

Soccer is fast becoming what Aussies mean when they say 'football', instead of that poor excuse for rugby they've put up with so long. The reason? Well, some would say John Hoggart. He has more caps than anyone else in the Australian national side, and his theatrical style of play guarantees happy crowds wherever he plays. He brings a real freshness and energy to your midfield line-up as well, with good vision and pinpoint crosses to keep your strikers busy all afternoon.

JOHN 'LARRY' HOGGART

Dmitri Duval

Skill:	6	Last Season's Stats:	
Position:	Midfielder	Goals:	0
Born:	Toulouse 5/6/77	Yellow Cards:	3
Height:	6ft 1in	Red Cards:	0
Weight:	13st 4lb		

Pairs well with: de Carvalho (D)

DMITRI DUVAL

Duval has improved more than any other of your players in recent years, and his high standards for hard work and fair play have gained him many admirers in football. Last year someone tackled him and got a yellow card. But Duval thought it was a fair tackle, and complained so hard he got a yellow card himself! A talented centre and inspirational role-model for the younger boys.

Ben Parker

Skill:	6	Last Season's Stats:	
Position:	Attacker	Goals:	9
Born:	Harrogate 1/3/86	Yellow Cards:	1
Height:	5ft 11in	Red Cards:	1
Weight:	11st 3lb		

Pairs well with: Hoggart (M), Stevens (A)

Still growing and still scoring goals. Ben wrote himself into the record books last summer by scoring four in one match, all of them with his head. The last one was a real peach, considering hc was facing backwards at the time and still managed to lob the keeper! Lovely eyebrows, as they say.

BEN PARKER

Salvatore 'The Duke' Duce

		Last Season's Stats:	
Skill:	5		
Position:	Attacker	Goals:	6
Born:	Florence 12/12/72	Yellow Cards:	3
Height:	6ft 1in	Red Cards:	0
Weight:	10st 7lb		

Pairs well with: Frost (M)

Duce is your oldest outfield player, but you wouldn't know it from his unwavering enthusiasm for the striker's job. His right boot is still one of the best in the business, especially since his mum moved here from Italy – and into the house next door! She does laundry for him, and he scores goals for you. You wouldn't have it any other way.

SALVATORE 'THE DUKE' DUCE

Ian Leslie

Skill:	5		Last Season's Stats:	
Position:	Attacker		Goals:	5
Born:	London 10/2/79		Yellow Cards:	2
Height:	5ft 6in		Red Cards:	0
Weight:	10st 8lb			

Pairs well with: Wehnert (M)

His small frame and big head have made Ian Leslie legendary in the box. He is able to duck and weave around defenders with astonishing agility, popping up at just the right moment to nod lingering crosses decisively into the back of the net. He is still uncomfortable in the public gaze, which has made him unpopular with some of the tabloids. But he has feelings too,

IAN LESLIE

and needs a protective manager to keep him doing what he does best: putting them away.

Jed Stevens

Skill:	5		Last Season's Stats:	
Position:	Attacker		Goals:	7
Born:	London 7/7/78		Yellow Cards:	2
Height:	6ft 1in		Red Cards:	0
Weight:	13st 3lb			

Pairs well with: Bostock (M), Parker (A)

During any match, Jed says he only has three things in his head: ball, keeper, goal. Apparently that's all he needs. It seems to work, as Jed has a rare talent for spotting a scoring opportunity where there appears to be none. Sometimes he will be crowded out in the area, only to duck inside his marker and slot one under the keeper. Other times he will be thirty yards out and sud-

JED STEVENS

denly fire a torpedo into the top corner. Here is a striker at the top of his game.

Danny Knox

Skill:	7		
Position:	Attacker	Last Season's Stats:	
Born:	London 15/8/80	Goals:	12
Height:	6ft 0in	Yellow Cards:	1
Weight:	11st 9lb	Red Cards:	0

Pairs well with: Hoggart (M)

We've all heard the grumbles. 'All they do is kick a ball around. Why are these people so rich and famous?' Two words: Danny Knox. Since his kidnap two seasons ago (and if you've played the first *Big Match Manager* book, you'll know all about that) you and your star

DANNY KNOX

striker have had a special bond, and he is more devoted to his captaincy at Hardwick than ever. He has scored more goals than anyone else in Hardwick's long history. And if you ever need proof of his popularity with the fans, just look at the sales figures from the club shop: more of his shirts are sold than the rest of the squad put together. Priceless.

Playing Matches

Over a six-week period, you will make your way to the final by playing matches against other teams from all over Europe. Hardwick are one of sixteen top-flight teams in the tournament, and you will begin in the group stage before going on to the knockout matches. The rules for playing these matches are on page 22. If you like, you can skip them for now and come back to them when it's time to play your first fixture.

The League Tables

Remember, there are four teams in your group; so whenever you play a match, they will all play one too. Each time you finish a match, you will be told the scores from these other games. Just like in real life, this can change the positions of the teams in the group. If you don't know already, these are the rules for awarding points:

Win: +3 points

Draw: +1 point

Lose: +0 points

To help you progress in the competition you will be given instructions after each match.

Player Substitutions

At any time during a match, you can substitute a player. There's only one rule: neither team may do this more than 3 times in any one match. If you substitute a player, it's best to replace him with someone who plays in the same position (e.g. a Defender for a Defender). But if you use someone from a different position, you must subtract 2 from that player's Skill for as long as he plays there.

Injuries and Sendings-Off

During matches, players may get injured or sent off and must be removed from the pitch. An injured player may be substituted; a sent-off player may not! Injured players take time to get fit again, and this will depend on your team's Fitness score.

Player Recovery

Before each match, roll one dice for each injured player in your squad. If the number you roll is lower than your team's Fitness, that player has made a full recovery. If it's equal or higher, he's still injured and cannot play in that match!

And Finally . . .

You are now ready to begin your adventure. Solving the mystery and winning the much-coveted European trophy is not easy! So remember, if you don't succeed the first time through, you can always go back to the beginning and start again as many times as you like.

Rules of Matchplay

Here are the rules for playing each of your matches. It's a bit like match highlights – as you go along, you will see the important events of the match unfold. The rules are really easy once you get used to them, and there's an example at the end to help you.

1. Start with a fresh Match Sheet. There's one for each match, and they start on page 274.
2. Pick your team. First you'll need a Goalkeeper. Then you'll need 10 other players. These can be any combination you like of Defence, Midfield and Attack; but you must choose at least 2 of each. You'll probably want to pick the ones with the highest Skill scores, but you should also keep an eye on who plays well together (you'll find this information in Player Profiles on page 8). Remember: you can't use a player if he is injured, or if he was sent off in the last game.
3. Write the names and skills of your chosen players on the Match Sheet.
4. Add up the Skills of all the Attackers in your team. This is your Attack Skill.
5. Do the same with your Midfielders and Defenders (not your goalie), to get your Midfield Skill and Defence Skill.
6. Your Morale and Fitness will also contribute to how the team plays as a whole. Add together these scores and distribute them among your Attack, Midfield and Defence as you wish. For example, if you have a Morale of 5 and a Fitness of 3, you have 8 extra points. So you could add 3 each of these to your

Attack and Midfield skills, and 2 to your Defence Skill. Or you could add all 8 to your Attack Skill if you wanted! It's completely up to you. But once you have allocated them, you may not change them during a match.

7. You will be told before each match what the Attack, Midfield and Defence Skills are for your opponents. Write these in the boxes on your Match Sheet as well.

8. You're ready to kick off! The ball will start in the midfield, so compare your Midfield Skill with your opponents. When you start a match, roll two dice and add them together. If your number is higher than theirs, add **1** to your dice roll. If it's lower, you must *subtract* **1** from your dice roll.

Now look at the **Open Play Table** below:

Roll two dice	Event
4 or less	They attack!
5	Special
6, 7 or 8	Time + 1
9	Special
10 or more	You attack

A football match is divided into six sections of 15 minutes each, and these are shown on the Referee's Watch section of your Match Sheet. Whenever you roll a 6, 7 or 8, you'll see it says Time + 1. That means 15 minutes have gone by – cross off the number '15'. Each time you get Time + 1, cross off the next number on the ref's watch. When you've crossed off the number '90' the match is over.

You'll see that certain rolls mean one team mounts an attack. If this happens, roll the dice again and consult the **Attack Table** below:

Roll two dice	Event
4 or less	Defended
5	Ball kicked out – corner
6	Foul – free kick
7	Time + 1
8 or more	Goal!
	. . . now go back to Open Play

Whoever is attacking, compare that team's Attack Skill to the opponents' Defence Skill. If the attackers' number is higher, add **1** to the dice roll. If the defenders' number is higher, subtract **1**. If you roll 8 or more, you'll see that a goal is scored. But has it been saved? Roll 2 dice, and if you roll **lower** than your goalkeeper's skill he's saved it. Unless you're told otherwise, the opposition goalie always has a Skill of 4.

You'll also see that if you got a 5 or a 9 in Open Play, a Special Event happens. That means you must now roll two dice again (don't add or subtract anything this time) and consult the **Special Event Table**:

Roll two dice	Special Event
2	Penalty to them
3	Injury – your player
4	Card – your player
5	Free kick to them
6	Corner to them
7	Time + 1

8	Corner to you
9	Free kick to you
10	Card – their player
11	Injury – their player
12	Penalty to you

⚽ If it's a Penalty, roll one dice. 3, 4, 5 or 6 = Goal!

⚽ If it's a Free kick, roll one dice. 5 or 6 = Goal!

⚽ If it's a Corner, roll one dice. 6 = Goal!

⚽ If one of your players is injured, roll two dice – the number you roll is the number of the injured player on your Match Sheet. You can substitute him if you want. This might change your Overall Skill. Remember you may only make 3 substitutions in each game.

⚽ If a player is shown a card, roll one dice. If you roll 1 or 2, the card is red: he is sent off! You're not allowed to substitute him this time, so cross him off your Match Sheet. Remember this will also reduce your Overall Skill. Rolling 3, 4, 5 or 6 means a yellow card – but if that same player is shown 2 yellow cards in a match, he is sent off. (You find out which player has been shown a card by rolling two dice in the same way as if he was injured.)

⚽ If one of their players is injured, their Overall Skill drops by 2 points. If one of their players is sent off, their Overall Skill drops by 5 points.

Make sure you note down these events on your Match Sheet as you go along.

Here's an example to help you:

⚽ You have picked four Midfielders for this match, making a combined skill of 20. You decide to add an extra 3 points from your Morale and Fitness, giving you a Midfield Skill of 23. Your opponents' Midfield Skill is 18. Yours is higher, so you may add 1 to your dice rolls in Open Play.

⚽ Your first roll is 7, add 1 makes 8. Time + 1. Cross off the number 15 on the ref's watch.

⚽ Your second roll is 9, add 1 makes 10. You attack! You have a total Attack Skill of 17, but your opponents' Defence Skill is 19 so you must subtract 1 when attacking. You roll two dice and get 9, subtract 1 makes 8. Look at the Attack Table: an 8 means you score! Write the score on your Match Sheet, and the name of the scorer (you choose).

⚽ Your third roll is 4. We're back in Open Play now, so add 1 makes 5. The Open Play table says Special Event: roll two dice. You roll a 3 – one of your players has been injured! You roll two dice to see which one, and you get 9 – you look on your Match Sheet and it's Klaus Wehnert this time. He had a Skill of 6 and your best substitute Midfielder is Ant Bostock (Skill 5). So that means your Midfield Skill is down by 1; but it's still better than theirs, so you can keep adding 1 to your dice rolls.

⚽ Your fourth roll is 5, add 1 makes 6. Time + 1 again. Cross off the number 30.

⚽ Your fifth roll is 8, add 1 makes 9. Special event again: roll two dice. You roll a 5 – free kick to them. Roll one dice to see what happens – you roll a 6. They've scored!

⚽ Your sixth roll is 6, add 1 makes 7. Cross off 45 on the ref's watch. That means it's half-time, and the score is one-all.

You play the second half in exactly the same way – and that's all there is to it! Whenever you win a match, add **1** to your Morale because of the feel-good factor. Whenever you lose a match, you lose **1** Morale.

Let the Game Begin!

What is it about Europe that has all football managers foaming at the mouth? Is it the pride at knowing club football is being played at its natural home? Is it the thrill of playing the game at its highest level, against some of the worthiest opponents on the planet? No. Let's be honest: it's the sheer elation, the life-affirming *kick* you get from knowing that, if you win, you're not just the best team in your own little country: you're the best club side on the whole damn continent. And don't let anyone tell you otherwise.

Well, that's why you're here, right? Why else would you be sitting in this dugout in eastern Latvia, wrapped up tightly against a keen wind that is whipping through the small stadium of FK Mazskaja and biting the faces of your hundred or so supporters behind the goal at the clocktower end? Happily for you, the weather's the last thing on their minds. Danny Knox scored from a solo effort just twenty-four seconds after the kick-off, leaving the two centre backs for dead and firing low and hard past the Mazskaja goalkeeper. That set the tone for the whole match. Ben Parker followed up just before the halfway mark with a decisive header from a Dmitri Duval corner, and Klaus Wehnert made it three-nil soon after the restart with a vicious pile driver from nearly thirty yards. Mazskaja have been tenacious enough, but they've seen all their efforts easily defused by Steve Fitzgerald and Carlos de Carvalho with some tidy defensive play at the back. The only player with nothing to do has been the Hardwick goalkeeper, Jamie Coates, whose bald head is looking decidedly chilly.

With ten minutes to go you're pleased to hear the home fans still in good voice. Although you went into this qualifying match as firm favourites, it's not every day they get quality opposition like you turning up at their ground and the sell-out crowd are making the most of it – even if they're at the wrong end of a three goal advantage. But they're soon drowned out by a clamour from the visitors' stand as Hardwick once more pour forward in numbers. Ant Bostock and John Hoggart are forcing the pace up the field with Knox out wide and Parker ahead. Bostock puts the ball right in front of Hoggart, who takes it without breaking stride. Hoggart passes to Knox on the left and keeps running; Danny understands precisely and gives the ball right back to him, beating the right back and opening up the defence. Parker is in oceans of space just outside the box, and you can see his face imploring John Hoggart to put the ball at his feet. Hoggart obliges, and Parker wastes no time in banging his second into the roof of the net, nearly taking the keeper's head off in the process. You clap your gloved hands together and smile inwardly. Job done.

```
        FK Mazskaja 0 — 4 Hardwick City
                    Knox 1
                    Parker 43, 82
                    Wehnert 50
```

Your team was gracious in victory, and you felt proud of them as they swapped shirts and shook hands with the opposition. That was the final match of the qualifying stages, and there were celebrations last night at the hotel. Your European campaign begins in earnest now, with all the glamorous excitement of the group and knockout stages to come.

As you sit at the front of your specially chartered flight on your way home, you notice a special buzz – something different today, a new confidence. Hardwick reached the quarters three years ago, but victory in the European League Cup has always eluded you. You lose yourself in dreams of international glory, and before long you're touching down on home soil.

'Just eight more to go, right, boss?' Zaki Roberts' mood reflects that of the whole team as he hops off the plane and strides towards the waiting team coach.

'*Exactement.* Eet will be a slice of cake,' adds Dmitri Duval.

⚽

It's Monday morning, two days before the first fixture of the group stage, and you arrive early at Hardwick City Football Club. You gave your squad a light week of training to keep them fresh for the match ahead, dribbling and ball skills mostly, and happily it was injury-free. The players have been getting on well together, and you've been content to let them enjoy the warm glow that comes with knowing that they're fit, focussed and fired-up.

The heating is turned up nice and high in your office, and there are biscuits and fresh coffee on the side next to a pile of post. All standard managerial stuff by the looks of things. You put one of those pink sugary wafers between your teeth and begin to flip through the envelopes on your way back to your desk. But the biscuit falls from your mouth as you read the first letter . . .

Storomere Testing Laboratory, Hardwick University College, HK1 7AE

Attn: The Manager, Hardwick City FC

Please find enclosed the results for the tests against banned substances (as defined by Article 23 of UEFA Regulations) carried out against the following members of your organisation.

James Coates	Negative
Robert Rose	Negative
Steven Fitzgerald	Negative
Antek Bobak	POSITIVE
Klaus Wehnert	Negative
William Frost	POSITIVE
John Hoggart	Negative
Benjamin Parker	Negative
Daniel Knox	Negative
Salvatore Duce	POSITIVE

In light of the fact that one or more athletes from Hardwick City FC have provided samples containing listed compounds in this round of tests, copies of this letter have been supplied to UEFA and the FA. You are advised to contact your governing body without delay to discuss the situation further.

Sincerely,

Jennifer Peacock

Jennifer Peacock
Head Technician, Storomere Laboratory

Your head is reeling. Is this some kind of joke? Not one, but *three* of your players have tested positive for doping. But how – and why, after all your lectures on fair play, the fitness training – don't they know the dangers? Not to mention the stiff penalties. Your mind is racing, it's all too much to take in. You stride out the door and into the dressing room.

'Frost, Bobak, Duce – my office,' you growl.

'You give us a pay rise, chief?' jokes Salvatore, but you're not in the mood.

'NOW!' you shout. A hush comes over the room and you glare at the three players as they file past you. You follow through the open door, and sit to face them.

'Well?'

'Well, what?' cheeks Antek Bobak after a moment.

'Well, what in hell's name do you call this?' you bellow, slamming the lab report on the table in front of them. Will Frost picks up the sheet and begins to read it aloud. When he gets to his own name he falters, stares at the page for a few seconds, then looks up at you. His eyes are like Pierluigi Collina's. There is silence, before he says in a small voice:

'What's going on, boss?'

'Santa Maria, I never do drug. It is a lie!' adds Salvatore Duce in a much louder voice.

You've had just about enough of this and you stand up from your seat.

'Are you telling me this is a mistake? That somehow the chemists have got it wrong for all three of you? Do you have any idea what this will do to the club? Tell me the truth someone before I do my nut!'

The players look at each other with a mixture of fear and confusion. Will Frost has let the report fall to the carpet.

'All I know is I never take anything, not even aspirin, without running it past Heather first –'

'Heather McCullough has been the doctor at this club for years!' you interrupt. 'What she doesn't know about medicine isn't worth knowing, so are you seriously trying to tell me she's made three mistakes?'

'Boss, I swear, we're not dopers. Something must be —' But Antek is interrupted by your telephone ringing.

'Get out, all of you. Report to me at the end of the week. And change out of your kit. You won't be needing it.'

You wait until the door is closed behind them before answering, but you're in no doubt as to who's calling. You have a short, terse conversation with David Woods from the FA who spells out the bad news — but it's nothing you didn't already know. UEFA rules state quite clearly that any player found to test positive for any banned substance will be suspended indefinitely pending an official inquiry. That means appeals, statements, not to mention the press — there's no way you can hide it from them. You hang up and sit with your head in your hands.

You instruct your assistants to fully brief the rest of your shocked squad, and stay in your office to think over this new situation. You still feel furious with the three players, but some nagging doubts have crept into your mind. They all seemed genuinely upset by the news. But was that just embarrassment at being caught? There's something going on here, and it's up to you to get to the bottom of it. And on top of that there's the matter of winning the European League Cup without three of your best players. Can you do it?

There's no time to lose: it's time to become the Big Match Manager!

1

Funny how things can suddenly look different.

Just yesterday morning you were sitting in this same leather chair, thinking how lucky you are to be manager of Hardwick City: at the threshold of a golden age and bound for European glory. Twenty-four hours later, the walls of your newly-decorated office feel like they're closing in on you and the smell of fresh paint is sour in your throat.

One gutsy centre half, a mountain of a midfielder, and your most flamboyant striker: gone, just like that. Cross these players off your

ALFIE STORRIDGE
1909

Squad Details on page 285 at the back of the book, as they're now banned from the competition. You're lucky Hardwick haven't been thrown out of the tournament altogether.

There's another problem. Will Frost was the only player who could play to any standard on the left of midfield. Losing him means Hardwick's width will suffer until you can get a decent left-footed midfielder – and everyone wants one of those. Make a note on your Fact Sheet that you must subtract **1** from your Midfield Skill in all matches from now on.

All this would be enough to make a lesser manager throw in the towel and admit defeat before the competition has even begun. But you're not going to let that happen.

You look up from your desk. On the long wall in front of you hangs the faded portrait of Alf 'Alfie' Storridge, founder of the club in 1909. He is holding a stitched leather football and staring back at you sternly from behind a huge bushy moustache. What would he do?

'I'm not going to let this stop us now,' you tell Alfie. 'Players come and go, but this club's bigger than all of them.'

You need to get your house in order, and fast. What do you address first?

If you think you ought to look at your staff situation,

turn to 252.

If you'd like to consider your own managerial strengths,

turn to 184.

If you want to think about drafting in some reserves,

turn to 74.

If you're not interested in doing any of these, turn to 271.

2

You're being far too harsh on your team. You might not like their performance, but it's nowhere near as bad as you're making out. Lose **1** Morale, **2** if you're supposed to have the Diplomatic quality. Now turn to 243.

3

What happened in the last half an hour?

You scored more goals than them?	(Turn to 204)
They scored more goals than you?	(Turn to 435)
You both scored, but it's still a draw?	(Turn to 391)
No one scored?	(Turn to 27)

4

You step gingerly on to the tile. Nothing happens. There is still absolute silence. You may now choose from the following tiles in front of you: the whistle (turn to 166), the ball (turn to 10), or the rattle (turn to 448).

5

You thumb through the numbers on your mobile until you find Higson's. It's still there, as you thought; perhaps you'd like to give him a call at home? If so, turn to 273. If not, turn to 422.

6

If you haven't already, you may talk to Antek Bobak (turn to 33), Will Frost (turn to 24), or Salvatore Duce (turn to 152). If you've finished your interviews, turn to 280.

7

Your players have a light workout and swim using the hotel's facilities, but you give them the afternoon off to relax. Meanwhile, you spend the afternoon working out your strategy for this evening's match. You choose a chair by the window in the lounge, with magnificent views of the old part of the city. There is a table nearby, covered in today's newspapers from all over the world, and you begin to clear a space to spread out your notes when an article catches your eye.

How did you deal with the group of reporters on the tarmac yesterday? Did you:

Walk on by? (Turn to 488)
Stop and talk? (Turn to 182)

8

Wednesday 15th – Match Day 1

You have had that familiar feeling all day: a mixture of nerves and excitement as the hours gradually tick away before the evening kick-off. The whole club crackles with an expectant energy, from the players to the ground staff. Everything is ready.

You enter the dressing room and feel pleased at the atmosphere that greets you. The players are warming up, pulling on boots and doing the private little routines that some players perform before each match. Zaki Roberts has to tie and untie his laces three times. Klaus Wehnert first puts his shirt on back to front. Carlos de Carvalho always phones his mum.

You greet them as you enter.

'Glad to see everyone remembered to turn up then!'

'Wouldn't miss it for the world, chief,' John Hoggart shouts.

'Glad to hear it.' You grin, pleased at the enthusiasm in your team. 'Remember, this is just the beginning of a seven-hundred-minute competition. It's a marathon, not a sprint, and I don't want to see anything reckless.' You say this looking at Steve Fitzgerald, who holds the dubious record of earliest sending-off in football history, which he got once after a two-footed tackle in the twelfth second. Steve holds up his hands in mock innocence, but he knows what you're talking about and you continue.

'Cover every blade of grass. This is our ground, and I don't want them forgetting that for a minute. Got that?'

The players murmur their understanding.

'GOT THAT?' you say, raising your voice this time.

'Got it, guv,' Ant Bostock says loudly, and the rest of the team add their voices in agreement.

One of the match officials, a tall man with hair as black as his uniform, knocks twice and puts his head round the door.

'All set?' he asks, and you nod.

It's time. Turn to 205.

9

That sounds good. Hardwick's Attack Skill is raised by **2** points for this match as your strikers aim to please.

Now turn to 365 to begin the match.

10

The hairs on the back of your neck stand up as you step on to the tile, but nothing happens. There is still absolute silence. You may now choose from the following tiles in front of you: the rattle (turn to 513), the whistle (turn to 277), or the ball (turn to 4).

11
Friday 21st – 1 day to the final

'Wake up.'

The voice is coming from directly above and you feel the point of a boot kick you in the ribs. You open one eye and see chinks of bright light around the blinds covering the skylights high above your head, and you realise you have been here all night. You feel sick and your throat is like sandpaper.

'Get some water and put him on that chair,' the voice says again. You are manhandled off the hard floor and on to a hard chair. A plastic cup of tepid water is held to your mouth, and you allow your groggy thoughts to assemble themselves as you drink.

You are still in Ventner's room, but the furniture has been rearranged to make space in the centre of the floor. Greg and Heather are sitting on chairs a few metres to your right, and standing shiftily behind them are two of the hired thugs who patrol this place with dogs. In front of you all is a large wide-screen TV.

'You'll never get away with this,' you tell them, trying to act defiantly.

The pair laugh at your cliché.

'Of course we will!' Heather says. So much time has passed since the tackle, who would suspect us? No one knows about Greg and me, and I'm trusted in the club. I'm sure you made quite certain no one followed you here, and you realise by now you won't be leaving any time soon. And besides,' she adds, pointing to the huge TV screen, 'we have a perfect alibi.'

Greg points a remote control at the set and it flicks into life. The picture is dreadfully familiar, but seen through a fish-eye lens so everything looks like it's reflected in the back of a spoon. It's

Hardwick City's dressing room, and the players are getting changed ready for training. The camera must be mounted above the lockers, out of sight.

'Who in their right mind would do this to their own brother?' Greg says. You see that Steve Fitzgerald is there in the crowd, pulling on his boots. In fact, it's just like any other day at the club.

'Has everyone arrived?' Greg asks.

'It looks like it,' Heather replies, peering at the screen.

'Then it's time.'

One of the thugs hands Greg a keypad with a display screen set into the top. 'I've waited ten years for this,' he says, his voice trembling with excitement. 'You're lucky. You only have to wait ten seconds.'

He taps a code into the keypad and you see that the display is showing 00:00:10. He and Heather hold hands. 'Hardwick will regret the day they ruined Greg Ventner's career,' he says, and presses another key. The timer begins to tick down. 00:00:09 . . . 00:00:08 . . . 00:00:07 . . .

Are you carrying a canister in your jacket pocket? If you are, turn to the number printed on the side. If not, turn to 110.

12

'This match has only just begun,' you tell your glum players. 'You wouldn't be blamed for feeling right now that this is the end of the road. But the second half is a different ball game.'

'I wish it was,' says a tired-looking Ben Parker.

'Think back to last season!' you enthuse, gripping Ben's shoulder. 'Who here has forgotten the final of this very competition, when an English side three-nil down at the halfway stage came back to level with the Italians in just fifteen minutes?' You grip Ben

Parker's shoulder still harder and flash your eyes round the room, imploring your players to listen.

'I've got a gut feeling in my stomach,' you continue after an impressively long pause, 'that this match is still ours for the taking. Does anyone disagree?' You raise your eyebrows, inviting a response.

Are you more than two goals down? If so, turn to 373. If it's not as bad as that, turn to 122.

13

Did you get more goals in this match than they got in the last match?

If so, turn to 372.

If not, turn to 217.

If you both scored the same number of away goals, turn to 241.

14

You curse yourself as you walk to Dr McCullough's office, but realise you have little option. All the serious medical supplies are locked away in cupboards, but looking through the desk drawers it's easy enough to get hold of a few basics. Needle, syringe, sample bottles.

Hope you're not too squeamish. Roll up your sleeve, lay your forearm on the desk and make a few fists to find that fat blue vein in the crook of your elbow. Now, the sharp pressure of the needle – hold some cotton wool over it to stop it dribbling all over the desk – and push it in, about a centimetre should do it. Hold it in place with one finger and extend the syringe with another, watch your dark red blood slowly wash around the inside of the plastic tube. Don't faint now. Nearly there. One more pull . . .

And it's full. You press down on the cotton wool to stop the bruising and cover up the puncture wound. After all, why would a manager be taking a blood test? You fill up the two sample tubes with your blood, half each, and dispose of the excess. You return swiftly to your office and use a felt tip to neatly print your name and club on the tubes.

Steven Fitzgerald, Hardwick City. Turn to 30.

15

You came so close, but unfortunately you'll never get to watch the final. The dog is keen not to disappoint its cruel master. It fastens its powerful jaws around your throat and does what it's been bred to do. Turn to 101.

16

Here are Liblonec Vyoslav's stats for this match. Mark them up on your Match Sheet as usual; then turn to 416 to begin the game!

Liblonec Vyoslav
Manager: Jens Kohl
Formation: 4-3-2-1
Defence Skill: 19
Midfield Skill: 22
Attack Skill: 23

17

You give your players a day of light training, concentrating on set pieces and ball skills. You declare Tuesday a day of rest, with time for the players to spend relaxing, playing table tennis, flower arranging – whatever they want, as long as there's no risk of injury. Your team is ready. Turn to 490.

18

Jamie is forced off his line by some good attacking play from your opposition, but he takes the ball comfortably in the air on the edge of his area. This time, instead of doing the usual thing of waiting for Hardwick to reposition themselves before letting fly into the midfield, Jamie takes his kick quickly. Most of the players came forward in that last attack and they've left themselves spread thinly at the back as the ball sails over their heads and falls to Danny Knox.

He doesn't even wait for it to bounce. With remarkable precision and timing he takes just enough speed off the ball by chesting it to the ground, then wheeling on the edge of the box, he clips the ball on the half volley.

The ball is on target and hurtling goalwards. It's all down to their keeper now. Can he pull the save of his life out the bag?

Roll two dice: Add **1** to your roll if you're paying Hans Gross to train your keepers, and add a further 1 if you are Instinctive, as this has obviously rubbed off on your players. If you roll 7 or higher, turn to 401. If you roll lower than 7, turn to 420.

19

Unluckily, the label was stuck down pretty tight and much of the address has ripped away. But you can see that the original envelope was addressed to someone whose surname is Ventner. And the first line of the address is: West End Mansion.

Make a note of all that on your Fact Sheet. Then, if you haven't yet read the fax, you may do so by turning to 248. Otherwise lock up for the night and turn to 527.

20

You pull out your recorder and press play. He stares at you, slack-jawed, as he listens to his own voice. But before it's finished he rushes you, knocking you backwards off your chair and grabbing the device. He drags out handfuls of magnetic tape and stuffs it into his pocket.

'Your word against mine now, "boss",' he sneers.

The phone rings.

'That'll be the testers,' he says. 'You idiot.'

Knowledge is power. Guard it better next time. Turn to 101.

21

'I'll call the police,' Nigel says suddenly, and grabs the phone again. 'Heather, don't worry, the police will understand, I will personally –'

'You will not!' Heather shouts, smacking the receiver from Nigel's grip. It flies across the room and cracks against the wall. 'This is MY family, and this stays between US. Don't you understand? People like this don't just stop because a couple of coppers start snooping around. This is revenge for something, and if I fail they will have their revenge on me. I will not have my family's life put in danger, do you hear?'

Hold on. You have a feeling there is something she's not telling you. Have you noticed any strange words Heather is using? If so, turn to 31. If you're happy with her story, turn to 193.

22

That means the mighty Homens da Guerra of Portugal will be your opponents in the next and final game of this, the most prestigious football championship in Europe. Hardwick will be there, and whatever happens now, that calls for something special. What do you want to do to mark the occasion?

If you decide there's nothing to celebrate until the cup's yours, turn to 138. If you take your squad out for a team-building meal at Luigi's, turn to 274.

23

You try the cabinet drawers one by one. They are all locked. Do you want to try smashing them open (turn to 222)? If you'd prefer to try the desk drawers instead, turn to 491, otherwise you can leave by the way you came (turn to 320).

24

'Frost,' you say loudly, breaking the tense silence in the dressing room. 'Come with me.'

Will Frost stands and shuffles out into the corridor. He hasn't shaved since you last saw him and he looks a state. You usher him into your office where he leans dejectedly against the wall, refusing to sit down. You speak to him honestly.

'Of all the people, Frost,' you tell him, 'I never thought you'd touch stuff like nandrolone.'

Is that a look of guilt that crosses Will's face? Sadness?

'What made you do it? Do you understand what this means for your career?'

'I don't know what to do, chief,' he says in a cracked voice. 'I need help.'

Do you want to try to make him tell you what he's taken since the Mazskaja match (turn to 113), or send him packing (turn to 6)?

25

Mulatta's manager wants 5 million for him. Is he worth the asking price, or do you want to offer less? First decide how many millions you're willing (and able!) to pay. Then roll one dice and add these numbers together. If the result is more than his asking price (5 in this case), your offer is accepted! Welcome Macaca to Hardwick and add him to your Squad Details (page 285). If not, your bid is considered an insult. Beware – you have only one chance at this, so make sure you offer enough if you're serious about this player!

If you have the Diplomatic quality you may add **1** to the dice roll as you have a way with words in this sort of thing.

When you have finished at the bargaining table, subtract any money you have spent from your Budget and go back to 248.

26

'We're looking at quality opposition, lads,' you say to your team when everyone is gathered.

'I am 'appy,' Dmitri Duval says. 'We 'ave to play the best sometime. Why not now?'

'We are the best!' Ben Parker announces. 'They should be worried about playing us!'

The players agree and you feel glad that you've been doing all the worrying for them, letting them get on with the football.

The first leg of your quarter-final match takes place on Tuesday 4th, five days from now. The second leg is on the Friday. You need to decide on a plan of action. Are there any holes in your team that need plugging? Do you want to shore up your defence, or sharpen your attack? The choice, as always, is up to you.

If you concentrate on crossing, one-twos and sprints, turn to 134.

If you focus on containment, aerial work and the offside trap, turn to 124.

If you want to work on avoiding being lbw or holed out on the boundary, turn to 145.

If you want to work on one particular player, sharpening his skills and turning him into a hero or playmaker, turn to 499.

If you like things as they are and go for an overall fitness and skills programme, turn to 88.

27

Oh dear. It's come down to this: a penalty shoot-out. It's the football equivalent of pistols at dawn: unpleasant, frightening, and something neither of you would do if there was an alternative. But that's what the last two hundred and ten minutes of football was for, and neither team showed themselves to be better than the other. So here you are, putting your heads in the lion's mouth, waiting to see whose gets bitten off first.

If you're not sure how it works, here's a recap:

1. It's a complete lottery. Don't be fooled into thinking some teams are better than others. It's a test of nerve on the day.
2. Don't tell your players that. Tell them: 'We've practised this, and this isn't any different to how we do it on the training field.'
3. But it is. It's like staring down the barrel of a gun. The goal mouth looks like the eye of a needle ten miles away, and the goalkeeper looks like a giant octopus with the reflexes of Bruce Lee.
4. Don't tell them that either.
5. Pick a penalty taker. It doesn't matter if it's a striker or a defender. Now roll two dice. If you don't roll doubles, you've

scored! Make a note of the goal. If you do roll doubles, the keeper saved it . . . shame. Do this now.

6. If you have the Inspirational quality, you are allowed one free goal in a penalty shoot-out. In other words, instead of rolling dice for a particular penalty, you can just decide to mark it up as a goal instead. That's because your very presence on the pitch fills your spot-kicker with confidence. But you only get one of these!

7. Now do the same for the opposition. Remember to give your goalie a good old-fashioned pep talk first.

8. If Hans Gross is your goalkeeping coach, he has spent some time practising penalties. This means that in a penalty shoot-out, you can roll 3 dice instead of 2 whenever a kick is taken against you. If any of the dice show the same two numbers, your goalie has saved it! (If all three are the same, he's caught it as well! This doesn't make any difference but it's *very* cool.)

9. Repeat this so that each team has had five penalties. If you banged in more than them, turn to 204. If they scored more, turn to 435. If it's still level, it's time for . . .

10. Sudden Death. This is just the same, but you review the scores after each team has had one penalty each. If it's still a draw, take another penalty. And another. And another – until one team scores, and the other one doesn't.

11. If your book is still intact after all that, turn to 204 if you were the lucky ones, and 435 if they were.

Real Sabadell

Manager: Rey Giles

Formation:	4-3-3
Defence Skill:	22
Midfield Skill:	19
Attack Skill:	22

REAL SABADELL

Make the necessary adjustments to your Match Sheet; the game is ready to kick off. Turn to 299.

29

Was it a score draw (turn to 292)? Or was it nil-nil (turn to 535)?

30

'The lab officials are here,' your secretary phones to tell you. 'Shall I show them in?'

'Tell them I'll meet them outside the dressing room.'

You are slightly dismayed to find that two officials have arrived from Storomere, as that will make it a little harder to switch the samples. You stride over immediately to introduce yourself, hoping they can't sense your nerves.

The older man has very short hair and a smile that flickers at the corner of his mouth. The younger has a wilder look and floppy hair that keeps getting in his eyes. Otherwise they look rather alike, and as if to make the point they are dressed in identical black trench-coats that almost reach the floor.

'This is Elliot Bastos,' the older one tells you, pointing at the younger but keeping his gaze fixed firmly on you.

'And this is Dylan Bastos,' says the younger, indicating the other.

'Storomere labs,' they say together, flashing their cards at you. You check: they're real.

The two are brothers, and it shows. It's going to be hard to put one past these two, but you'll have to try.

'Come in, please,' you say, and usher them into the dressing room where the players have congregated.

'Everyone,' you announce in a loud voice. 'These gentlemen are from Storomere and need to test your blood.'

'We have a list,' Dylan explains, taking out a list.

'Of names of players,' Elliot adds, scooping back his fringe.

'Shall I read it?' Dylan asks, looking at you.

'Please do,' Elliot says before you can speak.

The lab official reads out a list of six players whose blood will be taken. Steve Fitzgerald's name is second.

'Here we go again,' Howie Jevons says. His name was first. 'I'll have no blood left if this goes on much longer.'

Turn to 106.

31

What was the word Heather used that made your skin prickle? Take the letters of that word, and change them to numbers (a=1, b=2, c=3 etc). Now add these numbers together and turn to that paragraph.

If the paragraph you turn to doesn't make sense you must be barking up the wrong tree. Turn to 193.

32

Who is with you? If it's Nigel, turn to 216. If it's Heather, turn to 386.

33

'Bobak. This way, please.'

Antek Bobak follows you obediently and silently to your office where he sits and stares at you, unblinking.

'I don't understand, Antek,' you tell him. 'What made you do it?'

'Do what? I do nothing,' he tells you in his gruff Polish accent, still staring hard. 'What – you don't believe me? Then why don't you sack me?'

It's a good question.

'I play here for years, and you don't trust me.'

'Your blood was found to contain *nandrolone*. Are you seriously telling me you don't know why?'

Antek just shrugs.

Do you want to pursue this to find out exactly what he has taken? If so, turn to 360. Or you may dismiss him by turning to 6.

34

If you won by only one goal, or drew 0-0 or 1-1, turn to 227. Otherwise turn to 111.

35

At least there have been no injuries during the week, so you can go into this final match of the group stage with some confidence. Here's the lowdown on the opposition.

TEAM PROFILE
Kött Fotbollar
Sweden

Kött Fotbollar are the dream team of the Swedish domestic league, finishing top of their table by a clear twelve points last season. French manager Guillaume Moucheron is widely credited for building a midfield so strong it can control the flow of the game and stifle a lesser opposition. One of the bookies' favourites for the cup, this is a team whose pace and cooperation are more important than individual flair. Not that there's any shortage of that.

Star Player: Luis Covas
Left Midfield

LUIS COVAS

Watching Spanish midfielder Luis Covas play can be breathtaking. He plays on the left, but is equally good with his right boot. He has that sixth sense of knowing exactly where his teammates are, so he can pinpoint a sixty-yard cross to one as easily as he can perfectly time a back-heel into the path of another. And his own runs through opposition lines can devastate a defence as he skips, twists, turns and shoots. An opposition manager once instructed three of his players to mark Covas. He still managed to score. Twice.

When you've had a think about that, draw up your own team for this match. When you're ready, turn to 458.

36

You decide to devote much of the first week to your chosen defender, encouraging him to take charge of his back line and read attacking moves early. Roll two dice. If you roll doubles, turn to 49. If not, turn to 168.

37

Here are Kött Fotbollar's stats for this match. Mark them up on Match sheet 3 while your players are warming up.

Kött Fotbollar
Manager: Guillaume Moucheron
Formation: 3-5-2
Defence Skill: 18
Midfield Skill: 22
Attack Skill: 19

At last, the referee sounds his whistle and the game is underway. When 30 minutes are up, turn to 456.

38

You have one more issue to consider. The match against Revolyutsiya is at your home ground, so at least there's no travelling to worry about. That means you have two full days available to you to use as you wish. It's a management decision: what do you intend to do?

Put your team through two days' full training?   (Turn to 461)
Train them today and rest them tomorrow?   (Turn to 17)
Let them do what they like and just turn up for the match?

(Turn to 178)

39

Management isn't all about football, you know. You could learn a few lessons in communication. The trouble is, without talking to the players, you won't find out all about the – well, that would be telling. As it is, you have failed your team. Turn to 101.

40

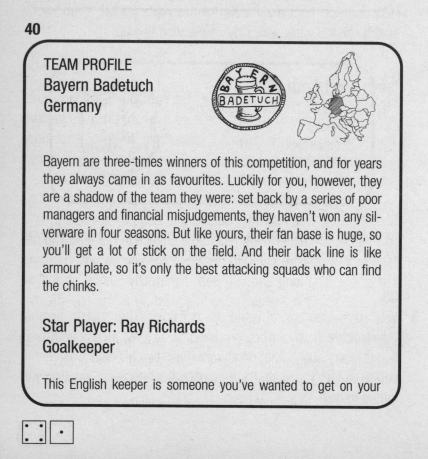

TEAM PROFILE
Bayern Badetuch
Germany

Bayern are three-times winners of this competition, and for years they always came in as favourites. Luckily for you, however, they are a shadow of the team they were: set back by a series of poor managers and financial misjudgements, they haven't won any silverware in four seasons. But like yours, their fan base is huge, so you'll get a lot of stick on the field. And their back line is like armour plate, so it's only the best attacking squads who can find the chinks.

Star Player: Ray Richards
Goalkeeper

This English keeper is someone you've wanted to get on your

RAY RICHARDS

books for some time. No one tell Jamie Coates though. The rivalry between the two is intense and bitter and they are in perpetual competition for the first choice position in the English national side. The two couldn't be more different. Jamie is dead safe and sturdy, and just has the edge at the moment, but he's slowing down in his old age. Younger rival Ray is showy and acrobatic; a walking ego but spectacular in goal. Needless to say, they hate each other.

When you've taken all that in, turn to 117.

41

Hoggart has made a brave run down the right, but he was too quick and there's no one in support. He does the right thing: he decides to go it alone, forcing a defensive tackle from the central defender. Hoggart goes flying over the outstretched boot of Meursault, and the whistle goes for the free kick. You wonder if it should have been a card, but you're immediately glad it wasn't; because John has taken the free kick very quickly and Ben Parker has run in to join him before either team has had a chance to regroup. The ball clears the defensive pack, the goalie comes out to punch but his reach just isn't long enough. Ben is perfectly placed on the far side, and rising in the air he nods powerfully at the ball. Timing, direction and power: all perfect. The ball plops over the line as defenders scramble in vain to clear it and, from a well-worked move by two cooperative players, you're a goal to the good.

Mark it up on your Match Sheet! That was impressive! Then follow the match to its conclusion. When it's all over turn to 384.

42

Tuesday 11th – Match Day 6

> ### Liblonec Vyoslav
> Manager: Jens Kohl
> Formation: 4-3-2-1
> Defence Skill: 20
> Midfield Skill: 22
> Attack Skill: 25

When you've copied this information on to Match Sheet 6, turn to 419 to begin the game.

43

Bingo. You hold up the glass to the light and there in front of you, clear as a bell, is a full set of Steve Fitzgerald's fingerprints from his right hand. Turn to 323.

44

Turn to 465.

45

The web page is a transcript of a tabloid newspaper article from ten years ago. 'Ventner's Future in Doubt,' the heading reads.

In today's European Cup qualifier, Hardwick City defender Greg Ventner suffered what could turn out to be a career-threatening injury. Latest reports suggest his right foot and ankle have been badly broken. If this is confirmed he will certainly miss the rest of the season.

The report goes on to describe how Ventner mistimed a tackle on a very hard pitch in northern Spain and his bone was 'heard to crack loudly' by other players on the field.

You all cringe together as you read this information. The report goes on to describe how the tackle led to a goal scored against Hardwick from the resulting free kick, which cost them their place in the cup that year.

Other pages tell the same story, and one follow-up article a year later mentions that Ventner was on loan from Hardwick City to a club in a much lower league. After that the news dries up completely.

Have you checked the Hardwick *Who's Who* yet? If not, you may still do so by turning to 245. If you'd rather look up the name in the phone book, turn to 112. If you've finished panning for gold, turn to 542.

46

What you said may or may not be reasonable, but the players all agree afterwards that it was rather out of character and wonder what's got into you.

You must subtract **1** from your Morale for this outburst. Try to be more consistent in future, and turn to 236.

47

Could Nigel really have bugged your office? The thought gives you goose bumps, but it just doesn't quite make sense. If he was the voice on the tape, ushering someone into his office, and they were listening to you in secret – well, your voice would never have found its way back to you. After all, you didn't bug Nigel's office, did you? And anyway you've never seen him use chewing gum in his life. Go back to 441 and think again.

48

The iron handle burns into your grip, but you don't feel the pain. The door flies open and you fall into a pile of leaves, and take blissful lungfuls of fresh morning air. You did it! You're free. The sun is shining, the birds are singing, and the caretaker watches, gobsmacked, as a sooty-haired lunatic in a shredded suit carries half-burned boxes across the car park.

Turn to 340 and remember to change your clothes when you get there.

49

Your player of choice reacts remarkably well to receiving such special attention, and the team as a whole will be buoyed by his presence on the field. Add **2** to his Skill and **1** to Morale, then turn to 278.

50

The other match in Group B finished as follows:

```
Kött Fotbollar 2 — 1 Bayern Badetuch
```

That means three points for Kött Fotbollar for their win, but no points yet for Bayern.

First, record Hardwick's result on your Fact Sheet (page 282).

Next, you should complete the following table to find out where you stand at this early stage. The team with the most points goes top of the table. If two teams have the same number of points, put the one with the best Goal Difference (GD) first.

Group B	Played	Won	Drawn	Lost	GD	Points
	1					
	1					
	1					
	1					

Goal Difference = Goals For – Goals Against

Remember there are still two matches to go!

When you're ready, turn to 329.

51

As a result of your excellent efforts, two of your players have achieved a new level of skill. Pick up a pencil and turn to your Squad Details. Now close your eyes and pick a player at random; you may add **1** to his Skill. Do this for one more player.

All set? Turn to 411.

52

Football's not about winning, it's about taking part, and – oh, who are you trying to kid? It is about winning: they did, you didn't. No points today. Better go and fill in the Group Table by turning to 89.

53

You open the door into a large bedroom. But it's the oddest bedroom you've ever seen. For a start, the walls are all painted gloss black, giving the dizzying impression that the room is filled with oil. The bed is made of twisted iron, with a menacing spike at each corner. On one of these a football has been burst, and its skin hangs limply. Littering the floor are newspaper cuttings – back pages mostly, all football stories. Several dozen more have been carefully cut out and stuck to the wall, and you notice that these are all reports of Hardwick City's results and misfortunes over the last season. There are even some pictures of you there, blown up to full size. But the really chilling thing is right in front of you. It's a table football set, the sort you get in bars. One set of players have been carefully painted in Hardwick's own colours, and miniature faces of each of your team's players stuck over theirs. But three of

them – Will, Salvatore and Antek – have had their heads removed, and you see that they are carefully lined up along one side, mounted on matchsticks like a miniature Traitors' Gate.

Then you notice the other team. Each player has been coated with the same thick, black gloss paint that you have seen all over this hellish home. And stuck to the head of all eleven of them is the same grinning face as the one that looked out at you from the Hardwick *Who's Who* nearly two weeks ago.

It's the same face that now looks up at you from behind a computer screen in the corner.

'Welcome to my den,' it says, nearly making you jump out of your skin. 'I wondered if we'd be seeing you.'

Turn to 93.

54

Taking plenty of time so you are not seen, you move silently up the grass verge at the side of the drive. On your right is a dark hedge, and you are careful to move as close to it as possible. In the half-light you feel sure you must be nearly invisible. To your right is a grassy area with fruit trees, and a row of silver birches screens the house and grounds from the road. Their trunks glow eerily white.

It takes several minutes to reach the top of the drive. When you get there you look behind you and realise it's nearly pitch black. Apart from a thin slice of low moon, the only light comes from behind the curtains of an upstairs window, glowing a fierce orange against the leading.

You stand in front of the main entrance to the mansion. The door is painted blue with ironwork picked out in glossy black. It's locked, of course. On the right is a bell-pull, the old-fashioned kind on a long iron handle. On the left a small electronic panel has been set into the wall.

Do you try the panel (turn to 195), or ring the bell (turn to 469)?

55

You conceal yourself in dense shrubbery and pray that the dogs don't smell you. You hear them pass nearby, but an unsuspecting cat on a night crawl distracts them and they go barking and bounding in the opposite direction.

Poor cat. When you decide the coast is clear again, make your way back to the front door and make the other choice. Turn to 195.

56

This is what the experts are saying about Liblonec Vyoslav:

TEAM PROFILE
Liblonec Vyoslav
Czech Republic

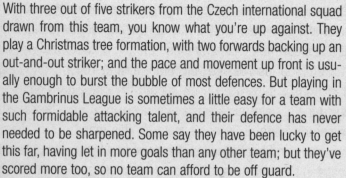

With three out of five strikers from the Czech international squad drawn from this team, you know what you're up against. They play a Christmas tree formation, with two forwards backing up an out-and-out striker; and the pace and movement up front is usually enough to burst the bubble of most defences. But playing in the Gambrinus League is sometimes a little easy for a team with such formidable attacking talent, and their defence has never needed to be sharpened. Some say they have been lucky to get this far, having let in more goals than any other team; but they've scored more too, so no team can afford to be off guard.

Star Player: Tomas Drnas
Centre Forward

Drnas signed for Liblonec Vyoslav four years ago, aged just seventeen. In his first match, he took the ball from the centre spot, drove it up the centre of the pitch, beat the entire defence and lashed in a shot from twenty-five yards. Since that day he's averaged a goal every two games, his value has gone up tenfold and he is rumoured to be the most highly paid player in eastern Europe. No one ever suggests he's overpaid.

TOMAS DRNAS

Select your own team now. When you've done that, turn to 42.

57

You press your finger against the screen. There is a soft electrical click from behind the panel, and after a second or two the words 'ACCESS DENIED' glow out in dull red letters. Then you are blinded as spotlights instantly illuminate the grounds of the house. Alarms are whooping from all sides, and you are so disorientated that you don't hear the men who stride up behind you and knock you unconscious.

That's as far as you'll get this time. Turn to 101.

58

Here are Lazzaro di Savena's stats for this match. Mark them up on your Match Sheet as usual; then turn to 416 to begin the game!

Lazzaro di Savena

Manager: Filipo Berlotti
Formation: 4-4-2
Defence Skill: 21
Midfield Skill: 20
Attack Skill: 17

59

Roll one dice and subtract it from Jevons' current Skill. You may sell him immediately for this number (in millions) if you wish. If you do, remember to add the money to your Budget!

Now go back to 248.

60

Your master plan is nothing short of perfect! Your players will respond better than you'd hoped, and this will give you a special benefit in the next **two** matches only. You now have **5** points which you may divide as you wish between your Defence skill and your Midfield skill. For example, you may wish to add 4 to your Defence and 1 to your Midfield. Note that this does not permanently increase the skill of any of your players.

Make a note of that on your next two Match Sheets and turn to 278.

61

The referee checks both teams are ready and gets proceedings underway. Play out the match in the usual way. When you reach the 30th minute, turn to 385.

62

You climb to the executive floor and find Nigel's office door open. He is on the phone, so you wait outside, but when he sees you he beckons you in and indicates a chair.

'Ah, how good to see you,' he says warmly when he puts the phone down, holding out his hand to shake. There's a bit of a mix-up as you automatically hold out your right hand only to realise he is holding out his left, and you blush slightly as you have to change hands. You're still wondering why as he sits back in his seat with a broad smile on his face.

Nigel couldn't be more different to Victor. He is young, fit, doesn't drink or smoke, and has Hardwick firmly at the top of his priorities. He used to work for his father when he was manager of Dundee United, and as a result he has a very hands-on approach to the team.

'Three of our best players, out. We're in a rather difficult situa-

tion,' he says, and you nod in agreement. 'I imagine you've got some changes in mind. What's the plan?'

He listens, nodding as you explain how you spent the morning, the ideas you have for training and the nervous state of some of the players.

'We need them to concentrate on the games,' he says after a moment. 'I think we should protect them from all this as much as we can. Leave the worrying to us.'

How nice to have a chairman with such an inclusive attitude! You agree to keep him involved every step of the way. He shakes your left hand again as you leave. Turn to 38.

63

You stop in front of the eager journalists as your players file past behind you.

'Ladies and gentlemen, how lovely to see so many of you, and my apologies for not talking with you sooner. I'm sure you can imagine how busy we've all been recently.'

You beam at them professionally.

'Who would like to start?'

The questions all come at once. The sillier ones from the lowest-class tabloids you ignore, but you can answer any of these if you wish:

'What's your position on drug-taking in sport?'   (Turn to 389)

'How are you punishing your players?'   (Turn to 293)

'Can you really compete without the Hardwick Three?'

(Turn to 237)

64

You decide the microphone is doing no harm in Heather's office, and she doesn't need to know it's still there. You take the second microphone out of your desk drawer.

'Of course,' you say, holding it out for Heather to see. She seems satisfied, and leaves the room.

Turn to 171.

65

Of course – Heather. Everything falls into place.

Steve was sitting in Heather's office listening to you talking. But your own bug is still in Heather's office – you never removed it! It was listening in too, just like Steve – and playing it right back to your tape recorder.

As for the gum, Heather chews the stuff all the time, and she was even chewing some at the start of that meeting. But not by the end. She must have used it to stick her bug under your desk when you weren't looking.

Your head reels as you realise you've been double-crossed by someone you thought you could trust. You know about Steve and Greg. They know you know. But what they don't know is that you know they know you know.

Got that? Let's hope so, as it might just be the only ace left up your sleeve.

Turn to 132.

66

'You might feel like we're in the ascendancy,' you boom, 'but that's what Goliath said right before he got an arrow in his eye.'

The hubbub in the dressing room quickly subsides as you speak.

'I'm a journeyman coach, and I've battled hard to get you here. I don't want to be let down tonight by sloppy passing or a defence that's half asleep. As soon as you get out there tonight I expect a force 9 gale on the Richter scale. And if you strikers do what you're capable of, I want to get a complaint from the RSPCG.'

'What's the RSPCG, boss?' John Hoggart asks.

'The Royal Society for the Prevention of Cruelty to Goalkeepers.'

Most of the players laugh, except for Jamie Coates and Rob Rose who are in discussion about whether the RSPCG really exists and they should join.

Good speech. Roll a dice: if you roll 4–6 you may add **1** Morale. Add **1** to your roll if you have the Assertive quality.

Now send them out to get warmed up by turning to 37.

67

The home team is expected to win, and they did exactly that today. You now have to make sure you can at least mirror their score when you play them at home on Friday. The pressure's on; but isn't that when you're at your managerial best? Carry the score over to your next Match Sheet and turn to 324.

68

You think over what the players have said, but there's nothing that would suggest that their odd behaviour is down to anything other than their own stupidity at taking a prohibited drug in the first place, and the embarrassment of being caught red-handed. Who wants cheats on their side anyway? You're just going to have to try to win this competition without them. Turn to 422.

69

You work the players hard, and you may add **1** to your Fitness score. But this is a risky decision so soon before a match and could result in injuries. Roll one dice. If you have Fiona Turner on your staff, subtract **1** from your dice roll.

If you roll 1, turn to 123.

If you roll 2–4, turn to 79.

If you roll 5 or 6, turn to 141.

70

The injured player operated in the midfield. For tomorrow's match, you may subtract **2** from your opponents' Midfield Skill because an inexperienced youngster will play in his place.

When you reach your destination, turn to 355.

71

How can Steve have planted the bug? He hasn't been near your office, and you always keep it locked. Go back to 441 and think again.

72

OK, here goes. You pick up the swivel chair and swing it against the locking mechanism of the cabinets. A loud clanging reverberates around the hard surfaces of the room, but you persevere and smash the base of the chair against the thin sheet metal again. The catches give way rather easily. One cabinet is empty. The other contains medical records of each of the players! You begin riffling through them, when the cavalry shows up. Two security guards – from the private firm that *you* hired to protect the club – are running down the stairs to investigate the noise. There are bits of metal everywhere, you are red-faced and panting, and there's only one door. You might want to be a bit stealthier next time. For now, your investigation and your career are over. Turn to 101.

73

Here are the opposition's stats. You will notice that they are stronger this time, because they have the home advantage. Copy the details on to your Match Sheet in the usual way. (Perhaps you've heard of an injury to one of their squad? If so, remember to deduct some Skill points.) When you are ready, turn to 404.

Real Sabadell

Manager: Rey Giles

Formation:	4-3-3
Defence Skill:	23
Midfield Skill:	19
Attack Skill:	23

REAL SABADELL

74

Losing those three players means the Hardwick City squad is down

75

to a skeleton level. It's too late to go shopping around for new players before the first match, but you still have a chance to draw on your reserve team, and even from your youth team. Of course, the standard isn't what you're used to, but then beggars can't be choosers.

Turn to 502 to make your choice.

75

You press the tiny speaker into your ear, click play and turn the volume up. You are so edgy that when you hear your own voice saying 'Testing, testing', you nearly jump out of your chair. There follows a muffled silence. Then the sound of a door opening and closing, and a woman's voice.

'You idiot, what were you thinking?'

You hold your breath as you wait for whoever Heather McCullough is talking to to answer, but then realise she's talking to herself. So she must have come in between the time you left late last night and the time you arrived this morning.

You reflect on how weird this feels, listening in to someone from the night before, when that person is in the room right under your feet. You hear a drawer being pulled open, and various clanking and rustling sounds.

'Thank you, thank you,' she is saying, again to herself. Then there is another silence, and the microphone turns itself off. Is that it? Or worse – could she have found the microphone? Surely she would have – but wait; there is another soft click and you hear Dr McCullough's voice again.

'It's me.'

A pause. She must be on the phone.

'Yes, it's all still here. No, no one but me. It's perfectly safe.'

Another pause.

'I don't know. I was just going to put it all in the boot for now. Yes – no, you're right. There's an incinerator on site. Much safer, yes. Look, I have to go, I only said I was coming in because I forgot something. They'll get suspicious. Ok. Yes, I'll do it now. Bye.'

The receiver is replaced, and you hear Heather let out a long, tense breath.

Turn to 530.

76

'Revenge?' you say. 'How do you know? Revenge for what?'

Heather curses herself for letting slip more than she had intended.

You lean across your desk. 'Tell me what you know,' you insist.

'I don't know much,' she admits. 'The threatening letter. It was . . . weird, as though this wasn't just for money or anything. Read it for yourself.'

She pulls a folded piece of plain paper from her briefcase, and hands it to you.

Weird is one word for it. This isn't just about Heather, or extortion, or even the European Cup. For some reason only they understand, someone wants to bring down Hardwick City, and it seems they're prepared to go to any lengths to do it. You're all in danger.

do you value what you love?
your instructions will follow.
hardwick let me down.
you won't.

Copy down this note on your Fact Sheet if you wish and turn to 193.

77

Steve's most recent call was to Greg. It was made just after the match tonight. The one before that was to Greg as well, this morning. And the one before that. They've obviously plenty to say to each other. So who on earth is this guy? You need to find out more about him.

If you want to try to get Greg's number, turn to 546. If you'd prefer to search for text messages, turn to 86. Otherwise turn to 318.

78

You might not be sitting pretty at the top of the table, but you're not lying at the bottom of the ugly tree either. Everything depends on your final group match, and you might need the Revolyutsiya – Bayern result to go your way as well. The Swedes are already through, but there's still second place to play for. Go fetch! Turn to 218.

79

There was one injury as a result of such hard labour. Pick up a pencil and turn to your Squad Details. Now close your eyes and pick a player at random. That player bruised his quads during a tackle. There's still a chance he could recover in time for the match though: roll in the usual way for this. (If you're not sure how, it tells you on page 21.)

Ready? Turn to 411.

80

Two games, two defeats. Teams have gone through from this position before, but not when the group looks like it does now. Bayern and Revolyutsiya both have three points, meaning that whatever the result when they play each other next week, at least one of them will have more points than you.

There will be no European trophy for Hardwick City this season. You're not going to find out what happened to your disqualified players either, as you're going to have to fight hard just to keep your own job.

Turn to 101.

81

It rankles a bit to take advice from someone you've only just hired, especially when he's telling you to put a midfielder in a forward's role. But you reason that Eddie probably knows as much about your reserve team as you do, with the amount of time he spends at clubs' training grounds up and down the country.

It turns out your new talent scout is spot on. Roberto Zapatero is thrilled at the news that he's being signed up, and he will fit into the line-up well. Write his name on your Squad Details in place of Paul Price. Zapatero will play as an Attacker with a Skill of **6**.

It pays to listen to all sides in this game! Congratulate yourself on your first piece of good management, and turn to 516.

82

Gutted. The Revolyutsiya manager is jumping around on the pitch and hugging anyone he can find, like he's already won the cup. But you can't begrudge him any of it: they won the game in ninety minutes, because on the day they were the better team, and you can't say fairer than that.

That's no points from one game, and things will have to improve if you're going to progress in this competition. Ever thought of becoming a rugby coach? Subtract **1** Morale for the loss, then turn to 50.

83

Turn to 434.

84

The players hold up their arms as the final whistle is blown. You applaud the fans on three sides of the ground, who are on their feet and applauding you right back. You can be sure they got their money's worth today, and you return, tired and elated, to the dressing room.

A win gets you three points: a perfect start to your campaign. Remember to add **1** to your Morale, then turn to 50, where you can put those three points into the table.

85

Saturday 22nd – Cup Final Day

Anyone would think there was no other news today. The papers you read over breakfast are full of your heroics, and as usual the tabloids get a lot wrong, having you parachuting from a burning building and Nigel cutting off his own arm to escape rabid dogs. Photos in the press show Heather, Greg and two of the thugs being led away for questioning, all with wild and terrified looks on their faces from the effects of the gas. You almost feel sorry for them until you remember that's what nearly happened to your own players. There are also photos of Steve Fitzgerald being removed from Hardwick's premises. He looks guilty and ashamed. Greg had a dangerously strong influence on his younger brother, and you wonder whether – in different circumstances – Steve could have gone on to great things at the club. He was stupid, but he acted out of loyalty and you hope the judge will be lenient.

You arrive at the club at eight thirty, expecting to be one of the first at that time, but instead the car park is awash with fans, reporters and staff. A huge cheer goes up as they watch your car turn through the gates.

'News travels fast,' the security guard says apologetically. 'I couldn't stop them.' He touches his cap and you drive through, feeling a little overwhelmed as you watch them clap and cheer your arrival. Well who wouldn't? You've cheated death again and foiled another evil plot against your club! It's barely credible, you think as you open your door and step into the sunshine. The volume of the applause goes up a couple of notches, and you can't help grinning as you climb the stairs to the main doors.

'We've got a cup to win today,' you turn and tell the crowd. 'See you in Cardiff.'

Turn to 115.

86

There is a single text message in the inbox. You click your way to it, and read.

Either his predictive text is up the spout or someone's trading coded messages. Do you know how to decipher the code? Well, then you'll know what to do next.

When you're ready, if you want to look at recent calls, turn to 77, otherwise turn to 318.

87

Turn to 296.

88

You decide that Hardwick's performance so far in the competition speaks for itself. It's not broken, so don't fix it: all that's needed from you is to keep pushing in the same direction, with a bit of fine tuning here and there. What's it like to be as confident as you? Roll two dice. If you roll doubles, turn to 319. If not, turn to 495.

89

The other result in your group was:

```
Revolyutsiya Apelsyn 0 — 3 Kött Fotbollar
```

That's another three points to Kött Fotbollar for a romping win over the Ukrainians. It's their midfield that does it: tight possession, slick passing and good vision that must be matched to stand a chance of beating them. Revolyutsiya's midfield obviously wasn't up to the job.

First, note Hardwick's result on your Fact Sheet (page 282). Then complete the table below (you might find it helpful to check the existing version of the table at paragraph 50). As always, the team with the most points goes at the top of the table. If two teams have the same number of points, put the one with the best Goal Difference (GD) first.

Group B	Played	Won	Drawn	Lost	GD	Points
	2					
	2					
	2					
	2					

Goal Difference = Goals For – Goals Against

How many points have you got so far?

0?   (Turn to 80)

1–4?   (Turn to 78)

6?   (Turn to 548)

90

Keeping one eye on the timer, you slowly reach into your pocket and feel the smooth cold of the metal canister.

00:00:06 . . . 00:00:05 . . .

All pairs of eyes to your right are fixed firmly on the television screen. Greg and Heather's hands are locked firmly together, their knuckles whitening in anticipation.

00:00:02 . . . 00:00:01 . . .

You realise your timing will have to be perfect for this to work, and you wait until you feel the soft electronic *click* of the device in your hand. The moment it is activated, you reach to the floor and roll it under Greg's chair in one swift motion. There are two soft thuds as the ends of the canister pop off, and grey gas drifts out into the room in noiseless clouds.

'Where is it?' Heather screeches, still looking at the screen.

The gas reaches the nose of one of the guards first, and he slumps forward on top of Greg, who struggles for a minute before succumbing to the gas himself and keeling over sideways. The other man is clutching at his own throat, his mouth open in a silent scream. Heather has stood up now and she is looking straight at you out of the growing cloud of gas. She takes a step towards you and raises a pistol, but her eyes glaze over and she crashes to the ground before she can squeeze the trigger.

You hold a hand over your own mouth and move towards the door before the gas fills your part of the room. The last you see is the picture on the television. Steve Fitzgerald is looking at his watch with a confused expression. All the other players are still getting ready to train.

Just another normal day.

Turn to 306.

91

In the lower drawer are two cardboard boxes. You open them one at a time, placing them on the desk in front of you.

In the first are several plastic pots containing tiny, bright pink pills and labelled Hexabulin. But it's the contents of the other box that tell the sick, sorry story of what's been going on.

Inside is a stack of small square envelopes. Each is labelled 'Vitamin Supplement' in Heather's neat writing and has a space underneath for a player's name. Next to these are sachets of various vitamin powders. Finally, there is a small mortar and pestle, for grinding pills to powder. The residue is bright pink as well.

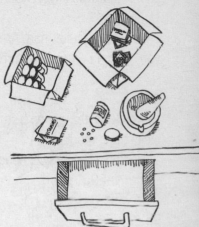

Turn to 140.

92

You're lucky. There on the bridge of the fork is a clear fingerprint from Steve's left index finger, and his right finger and thumb appear on the handle of the knife. Turn to 323.

93

Greg Ventner is still only in his early thirties and has the face of a young man. He is wearing a shirt and jeans, and looks almost normal against the backdrop of this House of Horror. But as he takes a few steps closer you see his eyes are full of hatred and bitterness.

You move to run as you realise the game's up. You've no chance of getting any information now and surely your only chance of getting out alive is speed.

'Stay where you are,' Greg tells you, levelling a small black pistol at your stomach. 'You've only just arrived. I saw you admiring my table football set. Fancy a game? Who do you think would win – Hardwick City? Or . . .' his lips curl into a smile, 'the Opposition?'

He's quite, quite mad. Are you here alone (turn to 510)? Or did you bring a companion (turn to 272)?

94

You pick up the phone and dial Heather's extension number. She picks up immediately.

'Heather?' you say. 'I need your help.'

Turn to 295.

95

It's written on a label which is peeling away at one corner, and you can see writing underneath. That means whoever sent it to Steve must have once received it themselves.

So someone's received a letter and then sent one. So what? But your mind is full of suspicion ever since the start of this competition, and you carefully peel away the rest of the label.

Turn to 19.

96

'The carrot at the end of the tunnel is in sight, lads,' you tell your squad just before they return to the arena, 'but don't get complacent. The game belongs to us, which means it's ours to give away. I want the same commitment as in the first half, same style, same content. Understood?'

Are Hardwick ahead by at least one goal? If so, turn to 362. If not, turn to 161.

97

You leg it into the dark orchard. Roll one dice. If you are with a companion, subtract **1** from the roll as you'll be easier to find.

If you rolled 3 or less, turn to 212. If you rolled 4 or more, turn to 55.

98

2:30 p.m.

The coach gets you to Cardiff in record time, as you have a six-motorcycle police cavalcade all the way. It seems like everyone is a Hardwick fan today, and half the drivers on the motorway hoot their horn at you. There is a special respect for you from the ground staff when you arrive as well, and although you're used to a certain amount of celebrity attention you keep catching people watching you and talking to each other in whispers.

'Are you surprised?' Danny Knox says. 'This match wouldn't be happening if it wasn't for you. None of us would even be here. You're a national hero.'

You are ushered into the suite of visitor rooms and address your team as they change for the match.

'Reckon you lot owe me one,' you say, and you wait for the laughter to die down before continuing in a more serious tone. 'This Portuguese side are some of the best I've seen on the international stage. I once heard that in hell the cooks are English, the policemen are German, and the mechanics are French. Well, this team is football hell: the goalkeeper is German, the midfield is English, and the strikers are French. I want a hundred and ten – no, a hundred and twenty per cent from all of you this afternoon. This is our only chance of silverware this season, and you've the weight of expectation on your shoulders. I don't want to go home thinking we could've won it if we'd tried a bit harder.'

You pause, and then shrug.

'But apart from that, it's –'

'A match like any other?' several of the players chorus together.

'Have I said that before?' you ask.

'Just once or twice, boss,' Danny says.

'Go on, get out there and impress me, you cheeky sods,' you say, and the players begin running past you. You follow them out the door and towards the noise of the crowd. Walking down the tunnel of light you feel like you're in a dream, and fleetingly you wonder if you've died and gone to heaven. But this isn't heaven. It's better than that. This is the Millennium Stadium. This is Cardiff.

Turn to 498.

99

Is Eddie Nimrod working for you at the moment? If so, and you would like to discuss your selection with him, turn to 242. If not, or you've never heard of him, turn to 235.

100

Think, think: was there anything in what they said that was common to them all? Something they all said . . . no, wait – something they all took? If there was any chemical, additive or supplement that all three players admitted to taking, that might begin to explain this mystery.

Did you notice? Was it:

An iron supplement?	(Turn to 370)
Painkillers?	(Turn to 183)
A vitamin supplement?	(Turn to 269)
Athletes' foot powder?	(Turn to 264)

Ginseng root? (Turn to 199)

If you're not sure, or you'd rather not pursue this line of inquiry, turn to 68.

101

Somewhere along the way you made a bad choice; or maybe you just had some bad luck. There is, of course, a second chance. Perhaps you'll want to be a different kind of manager next time; perhaps you'll want new staff, or a different team. It's your choice, as always. So when you're ready, gather your dice and go back to the beginning for another chance to be the Big Match Manager.

102

Wednesday 29th – Match Day 3

The week passes quickly and there are no major events. Jed got a bit upset when someone left a copy of *Geography for Dummies* in his locker, but he saw the funny side. All the other players have started calling him Sven.

You've only scheduled a light workout for your squad this afternoon, and the players can make a start on that themselves while you decide on your tactics, formation and team sheet for tonight's game. You are about to settle down to a couple of hours of tactical planning, when your secretary phones through.

'We've just had a call from Storomere. They want immediate drug tests from some of the players. They're sending a fax with the details.'

Even before you hang up, the fax machine whirrs into life and you pull away the emerging sheet of paper. You are informed that lab officials will be visiting in one hour's time to take blood samples from a random selection of players. Unsurprising really, and you open your desk drawer to arrange entry passes for the visitors. Did you bug the men's room this week? If so, turn to 529. If not, turn to 327.

103

What is the surname you think you've come across?

Winger? (Turn to 87)
Vango? (Turn to 514)
Ventner? (Turn to 153)

104

Congratulations! You've taken Hardwick City through to the quarter-finals of the European Cup! That puts you among the top eight teams in Europe. There were three other tables in the competition and they are all now complete: if you want to have a look at them, turn to page 277 at the back of the book. When you have finished, turn to 383.

105

'I'll join you in an hour. There's something I've got to do first.'

'Planning next week's tactics already, are you, boss?' Ant Bostock quips.

'You can buy me a juice for that, Asbo,' you tell him.

'Juice? Rock and roll,' John Hoggart says.

You part with your team at the main door and make your way up two flights of stairs. After today's news you wonder what Dr McCullough will have to say for herself, or whether she will even turn up. You wonder if you were wrong not to let Nigel Douglas call the police when you had the chance. After everything she said, can she have had a part in Steve's positive test results? You know she's under a lot of pressure, but could she really still be working against the club without having told you?

Room 105 is at the end of a long, deserted corridor, and the muffled chanting of some Hardwick supporters from the streets outside gives it a slightly ghostly quality.

Turn to 387.

106

One by one, the players are ushered through to medical by the officials. You accompany them and chat to the brothers as they go about their tasks with practised ease. Dylan is labelling while Elliot takes blood from the fifth player on the list, Klaus Wehnert, who is sitting in the chair trying not to look at the sharp point of the needle.

'So do you do much testing like this?' you ask.

'We've done fourteen visits this week already,' Elliot tells you with a proud smile.

'This is the fifteenth,' Dylan adds without raising his head from his work.

'That's a lot,' you suggest.

'Not really,' they say together.

With your two samples concealed in your palm, you pick the moment just as the needle enters Klaus' arm, and quickly knock the back of your hand against the neat group of blood phials being labelled in Dylan's tiny handwriting. The containers tumble on to the carpet. Elliot flinches and Klaus winces.

'Sorry, sorry,' you say, and hastily bend down to pick them up. You seek out the two with Steve's name on and switch them with your own, hoping no one spots the different handwriting. At least the pen was the same colour, you notice with relief.

'Butterfingers,' Elliot says without looking up, and Klaus closes his eyes tightly.

Corny but effective, and they don't seem to suspect a thing. When the tests are finished and the phials safely stowed in briefcases, see the men off and try to concentrate on the next match by turning to 35.

107

You fling open the door and half run, half tumble down the long, twisting flight of stairs that brought you here yesterday. You reach the part where the three flights converge, and below you can see the raised marble floor. You hear shouting and barking from above, and your heart somersaults as you see two men and four large Alsatians hurtling down the other two staircases, only seconds behind you.

You take the last half-dozen steps in one bound and race over the dais of symbols, taking care to step on only those you know to be safe. You fly past the pillars and fling open the door at the end of the hallway, slamming it shut behind you.

After the dogs bounded over the tiles they must have triggered an automatic switch, and the door has locked itself behind you. You bend double, breathing heavily while you listen to the cacophony of barks and curses coming from inside.

Then you smell hot breath, wet and sour. You raise your gaze until it meets the yellow eyes of a sleek black Alsatian, globs of saliva rolling off its fleshy pink tongue and pooling on the gravel.

At the other end of the leash is a tall man, his thin face heavily marked with cruel lines.

'Dinnertime, Keano,' he says.

The Alsatian bares its black gums and growls.

Are you alone (turn to 15) or with Nigel (turn to 421)?

108

Cochons d'Inde
Manager: Leon Orville
Formation: 4-5-1
Defence Skill: 24
Midfield Skill: 20
Attack Skill: 18

Make the necessary adjustments to your Match Sheet; the game is ready to kick off. Turn to 197.

109

'. . . three, Liblonec Vyoslav.'

The second man reaches into his bowl, and draws the opponents.

Sometimes you just have a feeling, don't you?

'Number one, Hardwick City.' He beams at the camera.

You will fly to Prague in the Czech Republic on Monday evening, and you can examine the opposition's stats then. For now, note the fixtures on your next two Match Sheets and then turn to 231.

110

You wait, helpless, as the timer counts down past two, to one, to zero. For a glorious moment you think the device has failed. But then you see a grey gas seeping from under the bench in the centre of the picture. The players sitting on it smell it first and try to cry out, but by now the gas is billowing around them. You see Jamie

Coates try to stand up and fall to the floor. Klaus Wehnert and Danny Knox are clutching at their throats, trying to fight the burning gas, but in seconds they are unconscious too. A few players have made it out into fresh air, but you know it's too late. The damage is done.

Greg turns to you.

'Don't worry,' he says. 'They're not dead. But they won't be the same again. And you can say goodbye to the cup.'

'In fact, you can say goodbye right now,' says Heather, and she points a gun at your chest.

Turn to 101.

111

There is a pause, and a lot of whispering behind hands. You catch the words 'barmy' and 'no wonder' – perhaps your response to the question was a little inappropriate for the circumstances? Lose **2** Morale as your judgment will be called into question on the back pages tomorrow.

Turn to 326.

112

You look up 'Ventner, G' on your online directory enquiry service. And for once, it actually finds the name you're looking for.

Ventner GJ, 11 West End, Calverton, CV1 8TJ

Well, that was rather easy. Now, if you want to check the Hardwick *Who's Who*, turn to 245 to do so. If you want to trawl the Internet for information, turn to 519. Otherwise if you've done all your reading, turn to 542.

113

'I need you to tell me truthfully, exactly what you've taken.'

Will thinks for a few seconds, picking at his wiry ginger beard.

'Iron supplement. Vitamin supplement. And . . . athletes' foot powder.'

'Nothing else? You're sure?'

But he has fallen silent and you know you're not going to get anything else out of him today. Turn to 6.

114

There's still time to go for a quick drink with your players, and you did promise them you would. Do you join them (turn to 508) or not (turn to 249)?

115

You don't get any peace inside the club either. The players mob you as you walk into the foyer.

'Not again, boss,' John Hoggart says. 'What are the chances of two conspiracies in three seasons?'

'Is it true you're going to be the next James Bond?' someone else says.

'*Formidable*,' Dmitri Duval is saying, shaking his head. '*Il ressemble beaucoup à Tintin.*'

'Come this way, boss,' Danny says, taking your arm. 'We've got a surprise for you.'

You follow him up the stairs to the first-floor dressing room. He pushes open the door and there are Antek Bobak, Will Frost and Salvatore Duce, all in the regulation Hardwick suits and ties.

'The calls came through this morning,' Danny explains. 'They've been specially cleared by UEFA to play this afternoon.'

Will shakes your hand and speaks for all three of them.

'Thanks for standing by us, boss. No one else thought we were innocent.'

'For a while I didn't know what to believe,' you tell them.

'I think secretly you believed them all along,' says a voice behind you, and you turn around. And although you know the voice, for a moment you don't recognise the short man whose piercing, pale-grey eyes are looking at you over a bushy black moustache.

'Higson!'

'I had a free afternoon. Thought I might come along for the match – if you have a spare ticket, that is.'

He raises his heavy eyebrows and offers his hand to shake. You push it away, and give him a bear-hug instead.

Even he wasn't expecting that. Turn to 98.

116

It's Higson's writing, and it's typically brief.

ENCLOSED:
PRINTING AND COVERT MONITORING DEVICES,
JUST IN CASE.
LOOK AFTER THEM,
I WANT THEM BACK
ONE DAY.
HIGSON

Good old Higson. Remember to thank him sometime. Now turn to 238.

117

It's only a short journey to the airport, and the bus pulls into the terminal in plenty of time. As always on occasions like this, there is another bus waiting to take you across the tarmac to the aeroplane. But as you step off the bus to make the short walk between the two areas, you notice that there is a bigger-than-usual presence from the national media.

Do you stride past and ignore them, holding your arm up to prevent them from photographing you and instructing your players to do the same (turn to 339)? Or do you stop and talk to them (turn to 63)?

118

Tuesday 11th – Match Day 6

Lazzaro di Savena

Manager: Filipo Berlotti
Formation: 4 4 2
Defence Skill: 23
Midfield Skill: 20
Attack Skill: 17

When you've copied this information on to Match Sheet 6, turn to 419 to begin the game.

119

'They say the away goal is lethal, but the penalty shoot-out is deadly.'

'I couldn't agree more. Look at the players. Have they got any more left to give?'

'Forget the players, John. What about us? I'm a bag of nerves.'

'Tell me when it's all over, Clive. I'm off to the bar.'

Brace yourself. It's the one experience every manager hopes will never happen to them; the one that makes heroes of goalkeepers and zeros of everyone else; the one that is, year after year, voted by fans and players alike to be a fate three times worse than death and twice as bad as public speaking.

It's the penalty shoot-out, cold and cruel. Do you know how it works? Here's a recap: read carefully.

1. It's a complete lottery. Don't be fooled into thinking some teams are better than others. It's a test of nerve on the day.

2. Don't tell your players that. Tell them: 'We've practised this, and this isn't any different to how we do it on the training field.'

3. But it is. It's like staring down the barrel of a gun. The goal mouth looks like the eye of a needle ten miles away, and the goalkeeper looks like a giant octopus with the reflexes of Bruce Lee.

4. Don't tell them that either.

5. Pick a penalty taker. It doesn't matter if it's a striker or a defender. Now roll two dice. If you don't roll doubles, you've scored! Make a note of the goal. If you do roll doubles, the keeper saved it . . . shame. Do this now.

6. If you have the Inspirational quality, you are allowed one free goal in a penalty shoot-out. In other words, instead of rolling dice for a particular penalty, you can just decide to mark it up as a goal instead. That's because your very presence on the pitch fills your spot-kicker with confidence. But you only get one of these!

7. Now do the same for the opposition. Remember to give your goalie a good old-fashioned pep talk first.

8. If Hans Gross is your goalkeeping coach, he has spent some time practising penalties. This means that in a penalty shoot-out, you can roll three dice instead of two whenever a kick is taken against you. If any of the dice show the same two numbers, your goalie has saved it! (If all three are the same, he's caught it as well! This doesn't make any difference but it's very cool.)

9. Repeat this so that each team has had five penalties. If you banged in more than them, turn to 372. If they scored more, turn to 217. If it's still level, it's time for . . .

10. Sudden Death. This is just the same, but you review the scores after each team has had one penalty each. If it's still a draw, take another penalty. And another. And another – until one team scores, and the other one doesn't.

11. If your book is still intact after all that, turn to 372 if you were the lucky ones, and 217 if they were.

120

Three matches played: the group stage is over. There was one more result tonight:

```
Revolyutsiya Apelsyn 0 — 0 Bayern Badetuch
```

This could be crucial to you depending on how many points you have, or what your goal difference is . . . Enough speculating. The results are in: fill in the table below, remembering to put the team with the most points at the top. It might be helpful to check the last time you completed this table – see paragraph 89.

Group B	Played	Won	Drawn	Lost	GD	Points
	3					
	3					
	3					
	3					

Goal Difference = Goals For – Goals Against

If all teams have different numbers of points, and filling in the table is easy, turn to 139.

If two or more teams have the same number of points, turn to 539.

121

The note is from your secretary, explaining that the package was left by Steve Fitzgerald. Steve agreed a two-year contract extension with Hardwick this season, and he's obviously getting twitchy about wanting you to know he's still 'on board' – hah! In the envelope are a wad of renewal papers bearing his signature; all standard stuff. But has something caught your eye about that envelope? If you want to take a closer look, turn to 268. If you want to read the fax instead, turn to 248. Otherwise pack up and go home by turning to 527.

122

'You're right, boss!' Danny Knox says, turning to the rest of the team. 'We can turn this around lads!'

'I agree,' says Klaus Wehnert. 'We can still get out of zese woods.'

'Chief,' Ben Parker says quietly, 'you're hurting my shoulder.'

You got carried away, and you let Ben go. But he's grinning at you and you're confident your message has been well received by the whole team. Add **1** Morale for a good speech and follow your players back on to the field by turning to 243.

123

You were lucky and no injuries were sustained. Turn to 411.

124

You draw up a training plan to improve the skills important in your half of the pitch. Roll two dice. If you roll doubles, turn to 60. If not, turn to 415.

125

How sensible. You don't want to risk any of your players having to sit out through injury, so you devise a programme of jogging, goal shots and crossing to keep them busy, with a couple of morning sessions dedicated to tactical analysis in the classroom. Roll one dice. If you roll 1–4, turn to 531. If you roll 5 or 6, turn to 51. You may add **1** to the roll if you possess the Tactical quality.

126

One player catches your eye:

Macaca Mulatta

Skill: 6

Position: Defender

Born: Buenos Aires 11/1/76

Height: 6ft 2in

Weight: 13st 5lb

Last Season's Stats:

Goals: 0

Yellow Cards: 6

Red Cards: 0

This is one of those footballers whose brains are in his head. Mulatta's as agile as a monkey on the ball, stealing it from the feet of attackers and intelligently dribbling his team out of trouble in dangerous situations. He's also got that rare talent which eludes so many defenders: he can pass.

MACACA MULATTA

Is Eddie Nimrod working for you? If so, you may turn to 187. If you want to bid for Mulatta, turn to 25. If you decide he has no place in your team, turn back to 248.

127

Australian Bruce Babel is a lover of languages and a football fanatic. Sounds unlikely? Bruce is fluent in no less than eleven foreign tongues, and having him in your employment means language barriers come tumbling down. In a multi-national team like yours this could pay dividends. Add to that the fact that you're playing in a Europe-wide competition, and Babel could prove to be a tower of strength when it comes to language difficulties with players, officials and even the foreign press. Welcome him to your club and write 'Bruce Babel, Interpreter' under Management Information on your Fact Sheet on page 284. Now turn to 480.

128

If there are any questions from the press you'd still like to answer, you may do so by turning to the relevant page number below.

'What's your position on drug-taking in sport?'   (Turn to 389)
'How are you punishing your players?'   (Turn to 293)
'Can you really compete without the Hardwick Three?'
                                              (Turn to 237)

If you've given them enough of your precious time, you may politely call a halt to proceedings by turning to 136.

129

Which of you is going to choose the staircase to take? If it's you, turn to 284. If it's your companion, turn to 32.

130

Who did you just defeat in the semi-final?
   Liblonec Vyoslav?   (Turn to 219)
   Lazzaro di Savena?   (Turn to 430)

131

You grab a handful of the packing material. Underneath are two more boxes, one slightly larger than the other. Accompanying them is a plain, white postcard with your name on it. What do you want to do?

Open the small box?	(Turn to 464)
Open the larger box?	(Turn to 162)
Read the card?	(Turn to 116)

132

You think back to the first round of drug tests. Bad enough at the time, but by comparison to what you now know it seems almost normal. You must behave around Heather as though everything is the same, of course. You wonder whether to tell Nigel what you've found out this morning, but knowing how his temper can flare up you decide it's not worth the gamble.

The club has started to fill with people, and outside your door you can hear members of staff greeting each other in cheerful voices. But for the first time, you feel utterly alone. Turn to 457.

133

Unbelievable. One of your own players, trying to bring down the club from under your very nose. But you've no idea why. Steve Fitzgerald has always been one of the reliable ones, no showman on the field but always early for training and as competitive as anyone in matches.

You know he's not working alone. You recall his phone conversation with Greg: 'I did what you said . . .' This Greg is pulling the strings. Presumably he's the one who wrote the blackmail letter to Heather as well.

You must think quickly. In less than one hour's time, Steve's nan-drolone-loaded blood will be carted off to Storomere laboratories for testing, and by tonight's match you'll be down yet another defender.

What will you do? You can try demanding that Steve tell you everything, but he might just come into your office and clam up — or worse. You could call Heather and see what she thinks. But can you really trust her? Could this all be a set-up?

Your choice. Do you:

Interview Steve Fitzgerald? (Turn to 308)

Interview Heather McCullough? (Turn to 194)

Get your head down and concentrate on tonight's game?
(Turn to 327)

134

You devise a plan of action to improve the abilities important in the opposition's half of the pitch. Roll two dice. If you roll doubles, turn to 223. If not, turn to 424.

135

'. . . two, Lazzaro di Savena.'

The second man reaches into his bowl, and draws the oppo-nents.

You knew it, you tell everyone afterwards.

'Number one, Hardwick City.' He beams at the camera.

You will fly to Bologna in Italy on Monday evening. You will have time later to study your opposition's form. Until then, make a note of your semi-final fixtures on your next two Match Sheets; then turn to 231.

136

If you answered every one of their questions, you'd be here until next week.

'That's all for today, ladies and gents, thank you. Now please be so kind as to let me get on with winning this match.'

You thumb in the direction of the bus, where you can see your players waiting for you. Wave your presidential goodbyes and go and join your players by turning to 517.

137

Both sets of players look worn out after a gruelling stalemate. You know that the Revolyutsiya manager will be far happier with this than you are, but things could be worse. You've taken a point from a match against what turned out to be decent opposition, and you should record this information in the table. Turn to 50.

138

Lose **2** Morale. The players are a little dismayed at how modestly you rate their achievements. Turn to 408.

139

Are you one of the top two teams in the table? If so, turn to 104. If not, turn to 543.

140

Why would she do this? The team's own doctor, who you hired personally because of her impeccable record in sporting medicine. She has her whole career ahead of her, a young family to take care of – it doesn't make sense.

You stare at what is in front of you, trying to force on it an innocent explanation, but there isn't one. Heather is trying to destroy the club. Then there are the players – the Hardwick Three, as the press is calling them – what must they have been going through these past two weeks?

Fury burns behind your eyes as you think about it. Turn to 438.

141

Such reckless enthusiasm! There have been two injuries to players during the training session. Pick up a pencil and turn to your Squad Details. Close your eyes and pick a player at random. He's pulled a shoulder muscle! Do it again. This one's broken his little toe!

Bad luck. Mark both players as injured. But there's still a chance they could recover enough in time to play the match. Roll for this in the normal way (see page 21 if you're not sure how).

When you're ready, turn to 411.

142

Well, if it's popularity you're after, go to the top of the class. Your players love you, and you can add **1** to Morale after having such a laugh together in front of *Escape To Victory* and *Alec Handsome's 100 Most Atrocious Defensive Blunders*. But you don't get to the top of the Europe tree by sitting around eating Pringles. Lose **1** Fitness. Now roll one dice. If you roll 1–3, turn to 436. If you roll 4–6, turn to 368.

143

Are John Hoggart and Ben Parker on the pitch? If so, and your Attack Skill is 20 or higher, turn to 41. If not, play out the rest of the match in the usual way. When it is over, turn to 384.

144

Homens da Guerra 2(1) v Cochons d'Inde 0(1)

Noordenhaarenijk 1(2) v Liblonec Vyoslav 3(0)

Lazzaro di Savena 1(1) v Kött Fotbollar 0(1)

First leg scores are in brackets, so add them together to get the aggregate totals. When you have finished, turn to 206.

145

That's cricket, you halfwit. Are you trying to be funny? Lose **2** Morale as you show up with a small red ball. When you've watched *Match Of The Day* a few times you may turn to 278.

146

What is it?

West End Mansion, Woodborough?	(Turn to 375)
East End Mansion, Calverton?	(Turn to 445)
West End Mansion, Calverton?	(Turn to 472)

147

Wednesday 19th – 3 days to the final

You arrive at work early as usual. As you pull into the car park, a security guard waves you down. You pull over and wind down your window.

'Morning,' says the guard, touching his cap in an old-fashioned way. 'This arrived for you first thing by motorcycle courier. Special instructions to give it you in person.'

He hands you a neat brown package and goes back into his booth. Turn to 164.

148

It's as you remember it. Just you, Heather and Nigel in conversation. But — wait — something else, right at the beginning. You rewind a short length of tape and turn up the volume. Two more voices. The first is a whisper: 'Quickly — in my office. And keep the volume low.' It mingles with the hiss of the cassette and you can't even tell if it's male or female. The second is much more familiar: 'Awright, awright,' Steve Fitzgerald is saying impatiently. Then a short pause, before you hear the beginning of your own conversation again.

If you haven't yet searched your office for bugs, do so now by turning to 240. If you already have, turn to 441.

149

Your training programme means your players don't need to be back until tomorrow lunchtime, which gives you the morning free. Any plans? Sleep on it, then turn to 506.

150

The press conference over, you say goodnight to the players who haven't yet gone home and head to your office to lock up. On your desk is a pile of post left there by your secretary. Among a load of junk there is a fax from the FA and a large brown envelope with a yellow note stuck to the front. What do you wish to do?

Look at the envelope	(Turn to 121)
Read the fax	(Turn to 248)
Ignore it all and go home	(Turn to 527)

151

All the medicines, sprays and first-aid kits are locked away in store cupboards. This is really just Heather's own administration room, so you're not surprised when you push down on the handle and the door opens.

You're standing in a clean, neat room with no windows. There are filing cabinets along one wall and a small hand basin in the corner. A desk with computer equipment stands in the centre of the room. You feel uncomfortable in the night-time silence and your own breathing sounds unnaturally loud.

It's unlikely, but if anyone came in you would find it hard to come up with an excuse for being here. Do you wish to:

Leave immediately?	(Turn to 320)
Search through the filing cabinets?	(Turn to 23)
Look through the desk drawers?	(Turn to 491)

152

'Duce,' you bark. 'Follow me, if you would.'

Salvatore Duce stands and strides out of the dressing room in front of you. He reaches your office before you do and slumps down, his angular frame awkward in the chair.

'What you want?' he asks crossly, before you've had a chance to sit down yourself. 'Already I don't play. My career it is over. You don't care.'

'I need to find out what's going on,' you tell him calmly. 'You took the illegal steroid; I'm the manager, so I need to know why.'

'I take nothing bad. It is a trick. The devil he put it on my pasta or *something*.'

'You know how tightly controlled things are here,' you remind him. 'No substances get passed unless authorised. What are you telling me?'

'You believe what you want,' Salvatore says, crossing his arms and legs. 'You always do.'

You take a deep breath. He's angry, and taking it out on you. But you still need to get to the truth. Do you want to press him for what he took between the previous matches (turn to 470), or just let him go and perhaps talk to someone else (turn to 6)?

153

Before you can begin pretending you have no information, Heather reaches across your desk and grabs the envelope with Ventner's name and address on it.

'What's this?' she asks inquisitively, showing it to Nigel.

'I was just about to tell you,' you lie. And you explain to them about the name of the envelope.

'It's worth a go,' Heather says.

Nigel is less optimistic.

'Where do you suggest we look? Yellow pages under "Blackmailers"?'

The three of you put your heads together and come up with the following. Where will you look first?

The Hardwick City *Who's Who*?   (Turn to 245)
The Internet?   (Turn to 519)
The phone book?   (Turn to 112)

154

Add the score from this match to the score from the last match. This will give you an **aggregate total**. Who has the most goals?

You?   (Turn to 204)
Them?   (Turn to 435)
The same?   (Turn to 378)

155

It's time to select your squad. No one knows your opposition's strengths and weaknesses better than you, so choose carefully.

When you've done that, turn to 211 to join your players.

156

Now Heather has come clean, you decide there's no reason to keep her office bugged.

'I nearly forgot!' you tell her, and follow her downstairs to her office where you remove the microphone from under her desk.

Note this on your Fact Sheet, and return to your own office. Turn to 171.

157

'Just this,' you say, bringing out your own cassette player. You place it next to Heather McCullough's, and watch their faces as you replay her little visit from last night. He is looking straight ahead, brow furrowed and mouth slightly open. She is wide eyed and staring straight at you, and the colour has drained from her face.

'This thug must have been hidden a tape recorder in my office. Stop this recording now – this is illegal!' she says halfway through, recovering herself and making a grab for the tape. But Nigel is having none of it.

'Shut your mouth and stay where you are,' he growls, and she pulls her hand back.

When the recording comes to an end, you pass the charred box to your chairman.

'This was in the incinerator this morning,' you tell him. You decide to leave aside your own little brush with death.

He pulls out the catalogue, the sachets and the mortar and pestle, which is still stained with a dusky pink residue. He pauses only briefly to consider.

'I'm calling the police,' he says.

'NO! DON'T!' Heather shrieks. 'Please don't.'

Her voice is full of panic and she has begun to cry.

Turn to 291.

158

The rest of the day went by in a blur. You and Nigel spent much of it in hospital for safety's sake while the police had sent squad cars and helicopters to surround the Ventner mansion. The men and their dogs had fled by the time they arrived, and the four you'd left in the bedroom were still out cold.

'That was nasty stuff,' one of the forensic team had told you. 'We're having it analysed now, but it looks like some combination of pepper spray, ether and hallucinogens. Enough to knock you out for a couple of hours, then make you think you'd gone mad for the rest of the weekend.'

As soon as you were cleared by doctors you were keen to speak to the investigator heading the inquiry.

'I went to get evidence. It wasn't quite supposed to turn out like this,' you explained from your hospital bed.

'We've got plenty,' she told you. 'The plot to poison the players is watertight, with or without your statement. That house was full of telephone numbers to help us nail a few other interesting people too.'

'And the drugs? Have you found any traces?' you asked, eager that the evidence will be enough to satisfy UEFA.

'Forensic are still combing the house. But McCullough's office and home have already been done and they reckon there's a pretty good case. No jury's going to throw much of this out, especially with the conversations you got on tape. If I was a lawyer I'd be advising them right now to plead guilty to every charge.'

She'd paused at that point and looked at you quizzically.

'If you knew so much, why didn't you just tell us?'

'I tried,' you said. 'Will you excuse me while I make a call?'

From your private room in the hospital you urged David Woods at the FA to begin talks with UEFA without delay. Saturday's match could not be rescheduled at such short notice, he'd told you. They were still deciding about the players.

'I think I'm ready to go home,' you told the doctor.

Turn to 85.

159

Have you had a conversation with former Detective Chief Inspector Higson in this book? If you have, you will have been given a number. Add the last two digits to this paragraph now, and turn to this new number. If you haven't spoken to him, turn to 345.

160

That's a great result. The away goal rule means you're already in a strong position with a home match to come on Friday. You can't afford to lose though, or you'll be out the competition! Carry today's result over to your next Match Sheet and turn to 324.

161

The team look at you like you've lost your trolley. Have you? You're not even winning and you're talking like the game's in the bag! Lose **2** Morale as the team have lost confidence in your sanity. Now turn to 243.

162

The box contains several components, each neatly wrapped in polythene. One is a length of wire with an earpiece. Another is a small cassette recorder. There are also two tiny microphones, each with a miniature transmitter. Bugging equipment! We all wish we could secretly listen to other people's conversations sometimes: now you can. But who? And what would a football manager be doing with a thing like this? Better hide it somewhere safe for the time being. When you've done that, make a note of your new possession on your Fact Sheet and turn to 238.

163

The door behind Greg is opening, and you see Nigel quietly enter the room. You're saved! Surely he's going to creep up and bash the villain over the head with a club or something?

'Where do you want this one?' Nigel seems to say without moving his lips.

'Next to our friend here, I think,' Greg says without looking round, and you realise that the voice came from the man who is pushing a pistol into the small of Nigel's back. Nigel mouths 'sorry' at you; you just shrug.

Turn to 510.

164

Up in your office you eagerly open the parcel. Higson has excelled himself this time. Nestling in a clear plastic box is something you've never seen before; and until today you weren't sure if these things really existed or were just the stuff of spy fantasies. It looks like the fingertip of a rubber glove, snipped off at the joint. But you see that inscribed on one side are swirls, lines and whorls, etched in minute detail into the material. You take it out and pull it on to your right index finger. As you expected: a perfect fit. Accompanying it is a typically brief note. 'Who do you think you are?' it reads. You smile at the double meaning. Below it, however, is a more serious P.S.:

Policemen never investigate alone. Whatever you're doing, take a trusted friend.

Good advice. But is this guy a copper or James Bond? Where does he *get* this stuff from? And how does he know all your measurements? But he does these things, and you feel very grateful. Make a note of this gadget on your Fact Sheet. (Well, what do *you* think it should be called?) When you're ready, turn to 270.

165

Here are the opposition's stats for this match. You will notice that they are stronger this time, because they have the home advantage. Copy the details on to your Match Sheet in the usual way. (Perhaps you've heard of an injury to one of their squad? If so, you'll remember to deduct some Skill points.) When you are ready, turn to 404.

Cochons d'Inde
Manager: Leon Orville
Formation: 4-5-1
Defence Skill: 24
Midfield Skill: 20
Attack Skill: 20

166

You wipe sweat from your brow as the tile takes your weight. There is still absolute silence. You may now choose from the following tiles in front of you: the boot (turn to 83), the rattle (turn to 311), or the ball (turn to 10).

167

The card is yellow, that's some small relief; but the ref clearly thought the tackle was just inside the box, and he is pointing decisively to the spot. Players come from all corners to protest, but he shoos them away like flies while he copies your player's name into his small black book.

Which player was it? Roll a dice for each of your defenders in turn. Keep going until you roll a 1; that player has been booked, so make a note of this next to his name on your Match Sheet. Now take the penalty in the usual way. If it's a goal, remember to change the score on your Match Sheet as well.

Nightmare over, or only just beginning? Turn to 302.

168

Your player of choice reacts well to your efforts, and his improved abilities will encourage the rest of the players. Add **1** to his Skill and **1** to Morale, then turn to 278.

169

The meal, however, is a great success. The players are on easy, relaxed form and there is a spirit of generosity and comradeship which encourages you. Teams need to be like this before all matches, but especially before the most important match of their lives.

The plates are cleared away, and you rise from your seat. You lift your wine glass (which is filled with mineral water, of course; what else?) and tap the side of it sharply with a pudding spoon. A cheer goes up from the table as they realise you are about to make one of your famous speeches. Better make it a good one.

'I never make predictions and I never will,' you begin, quoting one of your great footballing heroes. Some of the more intelligent players laugh. 'But tomorrow, I know one thing. Champions are not overnight sensations or a flash in the pan, but rather long-term performers. And I've always felt you were young men who walked the talk, rather than talking a good game without backing up the lip service with actions.'

'Get on with it,' shouts Dmitri Duval.

'Yeah, boss – are we going to thrash 'em or what?' says Ant Bostock.

You grin mischievously.

'There's no yes-or-no answer to that,' you say.

'I can think of two off the top of my head,' mutters John Hoggart sarcastically. Danny Knox pulls Hoggart's tie up to his neck so it makes him cough and splutter. There is more laughter.

'BUT,' you say, riding the team's good mood, 'over the years I have come to believe that I would rather pick a person's character over his right boot. And if I've ever had confidence in a team's ability to get a result, it's you lot. Cardiff, one week tomorrow,' you say.

Glasses are raised and a toast made to Hardwick City. Steve Fitzgerald is sitting directly opposite you, holding his glass up and grinning like he means it. And you're the only other person in this room who knows he doesn't.

Turn to 189.

170

If you haven't already, you may examine the note on the envelope (turn to 121), or pack up and go home (turn to 527).

171

Although you're a little closer to the truth behind the steroids scandal, you still have a nagging feeling that someone knows something they're not telling you. You've got this far using hidden microphones; perhaps you can get some more information this way. If you want to try, turn to 512. Otherwise, go on as if it's business as usual: turn to 537.

172

Then that's almost certainly what you'll get. Turn to 365 to get the ball rolling.

173

Even if you suspected Dr McCullough all along, you still don't understand her motives.

'Why, Heather? Wasn't this man threatening you? The photographs – your family – and you're working *together*?'

'You still haven't worked it out, have you,' she says with mock pity. 'Greg took the photos himself. A man of many talents, wouldn't you say?'

Greg looks affectionately at his girlfriend.

'It was all her idea,' he tells you. 'Once you gave her the job we were in. All we had to do was to wait for the right moment. And Steve was always going to do what his big brother told him. Blood is thicker than water, isn't that what they say?'

'And your family?' you reproach Heather. 'What about them?'

'You really don't get it, do you?' Heather says. 'I don't have a family. That was the nice, safe Dr McCullough we wanted you to believe in. And it was all going pretty smoothly as well, until Hardwick kept winning. And then you started digging around, so we fed you just enough information. We knew you'd come. You needed the evidence.'

'But why are you targeting your old club, and why those players?' you ask, determined to make Ventner explain himself.

'One from each position,' he says proudly. 'That was my idea. Did you like it? Rather neat, I thought. They are Hardwick's most senior players by the way. Hadn't you noticed? They represent the history, the very backbone of the club. Once upon a time I dreamed of being in their shoes.'

'Then why didn't you?' you ask.

'Oh, I'm disappointed. I thought you'd been doing your homework,' he says, shaking his head. The twisted smile has left his face. 'I'm going to assume you know all about the tackle, the one that left me strapped up for three months and in physio for another six.'

'That was your fault,' you say. 'You cost Hardwick the cup.'

'Oh, oh, I know, and *what* a silly, reckless, foolish boy I was,' he says, clutching at his heart and mocking your reasonable tone. 'But was what happened *afterwards* my fault?'

He's still pointing that gun at you, so you humour him. 'What did happen?'

'I was vilified. The press lambasted me, and I went from hero to villain overnight in the eyes of the fans. And what did the club do?'

Greg raises his eyebrows.

'Correct,' he says, not waiting for your answer. 'Nothing. They let me go; discarded me like rubbish. It took the rest of the season to heal properly, and I needed months of special training to get back on form again. But Hardwick didn't give me any of that; no, all they were concerned with was winning matches. As soon as I was back at the club I was put on the transfer list, but no one wanted me. I wasn't performing, and anyway things had changed. There was no room for me in the new system. I sat on the bench for six months before getting loaned to Arno Vale, two divisions down. I never climbed back up again.'

He looks genuinely forlorn, and you feel a flicker of real sympathy for him. His whole future changed, just for one bad tackle. You feel angry at the club for not treating him better all that time ago.

'You didn't deserve that, I agree,' you tell him, hoping he'll see reason. 'But that was ten whole years ago – I wasn't manager then, none of the players were playing for the club, and you're trying to destroy their careers now. How can you –'

'Hypocrite!' he shrieks, spraying a furious mist of spittle into your face. 'I've heard you in your speeches – "the cast may change but the script stays the same."' He mimics your delivery style. 'Well, you wrote the beginning of Hardwick's script. I'm going to write the end. And you'll have a grandstand ticket to the occasion. Sweet dreams, boss.'

For a minute you think he's going to let you go. But then an unseen hand from behind claps a damp cloth to your mouth and you smell chloroform. You gasp, and you're falling . . .

Turn to 11.

174

You made it! You are standing at the foot of what appeared to be a single staircase, but which you now notice splits into three part of the way up. Above that it gets gloomy and you can't make out where they lead. Are you alone (turn to 284), or do you have a companion (turn to 129)?

175

You arrive home thirty minutes later to find that there is already a message on your answering machine. It's from your chairman, informing you that you are being suspended indefinitely, pending an inquiry into 'inappropriate conduct'.

Your reputation is in tatters and your career is over. Turn to 101.

176

You ring Scotland Yard and ask to be put through to Higson's extension number. The operator obliges, and after two rings the phone is answered at the other end. But it is a female voice who answers.

'DCI Higson? I'm sorry. He retired six months ago. I'm his replacement, DCI Cudner. Can I help at all?'

You embark on your explanation of the drugs charges and the talks you had with your players, but when you get to your vitamin theory you begin to feel rather foolish. You struggle to make a coherent story, and quickly realise that you just haven't got much of a case.

There is a pause on the other end of the line, then:

'I've followed the story in the press and I know about you. I'm a bit of a football fan myself, as it happens. But I can only imagine you've been under a lot of strain recently. This just isn't a police matter, I'm afraid. It seems very simple to me: your players have been caught and must be disciplined. That's up to you and UEFA. I'm sorry.'

Cudner's tone is friendly but firm. You apologise and hang up, feeling a little embarrassed and rather confused.

Turn to 5.

177

'Number five. Real Sabadell, from Spain!'

You have seen Real Sabadell play live on several occasions. They are an impressive attacking squad with a very highly thought-of manager.

You'll learn more about them later. For now, make a note of this fixture on your next two Match Sheets, then turn to 380.

178

Your players have spent no time together and most of them have just lazed around playing computer games and watching TV. What were you thinking? Fitness is like a rare flower: it needs careful but constant cultivation, or it will wither. Subtract **1** point from your Fitness and another **1** from Morale, as most players haven't seen each other for two whole days.

Turn to 490.

179

You join the others at the table as they are finishing their starters. Between courses you address the table.

'It's been a tough time recently, for all of you,' you say. 'To be honest, I wondered if we'd make it this far at all. But we have, and that's in the face of all the pressure we're under.'

You pause, wondering how to continue without lying to your players, but without pretending everything's all right either.

'I've heard the same rumours as you have,' you continue, 'and I can understand that you feel worried for your own future every time you take a drug test.'

'You've got to admit it's pretty weird,' Zaki Roberts says bravely.

'I never heard such a thing like this,' Klaus Wehnert adds.

'But I can tell you all right now,' you insist, impatient to catch the mood before it darkens, 'that I am in close contact with Dr McCullough, the FA and the police, and I can say for certain that none of you is in any danger whatsoever and that the club will handle this matter transparently and professionally. I'm on your side.'

You sit back, looking around the table at each of the players, wondering whether you lied or not. You glance at Steve, and he is doing his best to look nonchalant. But seeing that your words have reassured the other players makes you twice as determined to investigate the strange events at Hardwick, whatever that takes. Danny gives you a small smile as if he agrees. But you wish you could tell him everything you know, and you find it hard to smile back.

Turn to 254.

180

Nigel suggests you take the left flight. Turn to 298.

181

What do you want to do? Clear out your office and drive home (turn to 175), or wait for Nigel Douglas to arrive and explain the truth (turn to 340)?

182

You will have been given points depending on what answers you gave. How many points did you get altogether? If you are Assertive, you may add an extra point.

1–4?   (Turn to 188)
5 or more?   (Turn to 413)

183
Turn to 526.

184
This is your adventure, and no one can tell you what to do or how to behave. As well as the decisions you make, the kind of person you are will also have a dramatic effect on the performance of your players and the success you achieve. Ever been told to 'just be yourself'? Well, what kind of person are you? Below is a list of six Manager Qualities. You may select a maximum of two from the list. To find out what effect each one has, turn to its paragraph number. But choose carefully, because if you don't like what you find, it's tough – you're stuck with it. Are you:

Tactical?	(Turn to 518)
Diplomatic?	(Turn to 503)
Assertive?	(Turn to 397)
Flexible?	(Turn to 479)
Inspirational?	(Turn to 455)
Instinctive?	(Turn to 247)

185
Oriol Aspachs' current manager wants 6 million for him. If you want to buy him, decide how much you want to pay in millions. Then roll one dice and add this number to your bid. If this total is higher than the asking price (6), then your bid has been accepted and Aspachs has joined your team! If it is equal or lower, you have failed. You only get one go at this, so if your bid is rejected you can't just roll the dice again. And you can't offer more money than you actually have!

If you are Diplomatic, you can add **1** to your dice roll because you're such a good negotiator.

If you buy this player, don't forget to subtract the money you offered from your Budget. Add Oriol's name and Skill to your Squad Details (page 285) and turn immediately to 417. Alternatively you might want more time to think about it. Whatever you choose, go back to 250 and decide what to do next.

186

If you haven't already, you may open the parcel (turn to 200) or the letter (turn to 459). If you've finished with today's post, turn to 337.

187

You speak with Eddie about Macaca and the current state of the market. He agrees that there's not much around.

'Except,' he adds, 'for Ursos Arctos, the Icelandic midfielder. He's not officially for sale, but I know for a fact that his manager is rearranging the team. If he gets his new signing there will be no place for Arctos in the line-up and you might be able to get him for a bargain price.'

Ursos Arctos

Skill: 7	Last Season's Stats:	
Position: Midfielder	Goals:	5
Born: Reykjavik 29/2/78	Yellow Cards:	3
Height: 6ft 6in	Red Cards:	1
Weight: 14st 0lb		

This bear of a man is one of the few Icelandic players to make it on to the international stage. He has two great feet, a right and a left, which means he can play in virtually any position.

If you want to put in a bid for Ursos, turn to 192. If you wish to bid for Macaca you can review his vitals by returning to 126. If you are not interested in either player, go back to 248.

URSOS ARCTOS

188

The Sports section of one of the British broadsheets is face-up. 'Hardwick Manager Breaks Silence,' reads the headline, and underneath there is a half-page photograph of you with the aeroplane that brought you here in the background. You hastily read on:

. . . answered reporters' questions at last . . . giving little away . . . Hardwick's manager was in buoyant mood but seemed a little cagey . . . still much we are not being told . . . Is the club taking the Hardwick Three seriously enough?

It could be worse, but the papers are still hungry for information and it's almost as if you're being blamed for this situation! Similar stories are splashed all over the morning news and you realise that the players are bound to get wind of it before the kick-off this evening. Lose **1** Morale as this is sure to distract them from the football. Now turn to 426.

189

At nine thirty the dinner is over and you tell your squad you will settle the bill on the club account.

'Night, chief,' Jamie Coates says.

'Need a lift, boss?' asks Danny Knox.

You decline and tell the players you'll see them in the morning. They file out on to the street and into waiting taxis.

You are on your own in the restaurant and sit finishing the last of your coffee as the staff wait to clear the table. You know you have only one week to get to the bottom of the scandal that has threatened to cripple the club, and your only chance is to get into Greg Ventner's house. But how will you do it?

Do you have fingerprinting equipment (turn to 321)? Or not (turn to 379)?

190

'Let's get one thing straight. Those three are idiots,' you tell your squad. 'They made their bed and now they're lying in it. They'll play no further part in this competition and we'll not miss cretins like that.'

You pause to let this sink in.

'Now tell me, do any of you lot have any intention of pumping your bodies full of dope like some macho, muscle-bound . . . freaks?' You falter a bit as you run out of insults, but the point is made. 'Because if you do, you can get out now.'

No one says a word.

Do you have the Diplomatic Quality? If so, turn to 46. If not, turn to 256.

191

Your plane lands and you begin making your way home. Your mind turns to the competition and the fact that Hardwick have made it through the quarters. There were three other quarter-final second legs played this evening as well. You can see the results by turning to 303 if you wish. Then turn to 206.

192

Eddie's inside information was spot on. Despite his Skill of 7, Ursos will be released to Hardwick for a mere 2 million! If you decide to buy him, add his name to your Squad Details on page 285 (remembering to subtract 2 million from your Budget). What a give-away! Eddie is worth his weight in gold. And not only have you got a great new player; Arctos' left-boot prowess means he will play naturally on that side of midfield. Your nagging left-side problems are over! You will no longer have to deduct 1 from your Midfield Skill; make a note of this on your Fact Sheet.

Now turn back to 248 to decide what to do next.

193

'You did the right thing,' Nigel tells Heather.

'We won't do anything to put your family in danger,' you reassure her. 'This stays between the three of us for as long as it needs to. But that can't be for ever. We need to find out who's doing this without their knowledge. We'll need to work together, in secret.'

'I agree,' Heather says readily.

'I suppose so,' Nigel says at length. 'We should meet again soon – say next Wednesday after the match, Room 105?'

You agree to this: make a note of the appointment on your Fact Sheet.

You're all in this together now. As Nigel and Heather trudge from your office, you realise with a lonely groan that you will have to go on pretending to Will, Salvatore and Antek that you still think they willingly took drugs. Anything else might arouse suspicion; and after all, who do you dare to trust now?

Almost immediately the door to your office is reopened.

'I just had a thought,' Dr McCullough says. 'That mike you got me with – pretty nifty. You have removed the microphone now, haven't you?'

Quick – make a decision! Do you lie (turn to 64) or tell the truth (turn to 156)?

194

You tell your secretary you want to speak to Heather McCullough, but you are informed immediately that she has gone home for the day. You try her mobile but it's turned off.

With three players already suspended, Hardwick is down to its bare bones and certainly isn't stable enough to lose another defender – even a corrupt one. But if his blood is taken for testing, that's exactly what will happen. If only you could buy yourself some time while you figure out what's going on here . . .

His blood.

Fancy doing something illegal? I mean, really illegal – the kind of thing that, if you got caught, would mean the end of your career and a probable spell in prison?

Yes?   (Turn to 14)

No?   (Turn to 327)

195

You flip up the plastic cover of the panel. Underneath there are no buttons; just a touch screen.

Well, here goes. Do you have a false fingerprint to put on? If so, turn to 440. If not, turn to 57.

196

Aaargh! It's like a penalty shoot-out, only worse. You're going to have to toss a coin to see which of the two level-pegging teams goes above the other in the table. Ah well, that's UEFA rules. Done it? Your table should finally be complete, and you may turn to 139.

197

The referee signals the game to begin, and the ball is kicked for the first time. Play out this game in the usual way. When the ref's watch says 60 minutes, turn to 143.

198

So . . . what happened? If you won, turn to 226. If you lost, turn to 52. If the match ended in a draw, turn to 29.

199

Turn to 526.

200

You carefully peel off the paper, hoping it's not a case of dodgy wine. It's not. But you're disappointed to discover the contents to be a box of polystyrene chips! Who would send a thing like that? If you want to examine the letter instead, turn to 459. If you empty the chips into the bin, turn to 131.

201

Occasionally in a football match, something happens which can suddenly swing the game in favour of one team. This time it's your team. First, the referee blows his whistle. Second, he points to the spot. He's given a penalty! You applaud the decision, and your two players: Ant set it up, and Jed forced the goalie to take the risk. The Hardwick crowd are sounding their approval, and some of them are letting the Kött Fotbollar fans know about the penalty in case they hadn't noticed.

Roll again. If you roll 1–3, turn to 246. If 4–6, turn to 400.

202

You went into this match as clear favourites, but Revolyutsiya have managed to hold you back in the first half.

It might be time to make some changes. You could always bring on an Attacker to replace a Defender; this could make scoring easier for you, but also for them! Perhaps you want to shore up your defence to stop them getting any goals in the second half, but this would mean losing a player from somewhere else on the field . . . Who said football management was easy anyway?

Whatever you do will change the course of the game, so remember to update all your Skill scores if you make any changes.

Now turn to 228.

203

If you won by two or more goals, turn to 227. If not, or you lost or drew, turn to 111.

204

You did it! When you started this job, there were high hopes for what you'd bring to the club; but this is beyond the wildest dreams of even the most optimistic fan. For the first time in Hardwick's history, they're going to the final of the biggest club competition on the planet. And who is this mysterious individual steering the ship? The world's press are going to want to know all about you after this, from *Manager Monthly* to *Hi!* magazine.

Yes, yes – but that's not what you do this for. From getting the job done, to scoring more goals than you let in, football is all you care about. Isn't it? It better be, because ever since the completion of the new stadium at Wembley, the Millennium Stadium at Cardiff has reverted to a neutral international ground. And since it's one of the best modern stadia in Europe, it has been selected as the venue for the final to be played on Saturday 22nd at 3 p.m., exactly one week tomorrow.

Put it in your diary. Then turn to 130.

205

You walk your players down the tunnel, which is lined with burly security guards wearing dark suits and earpieces. There are four policemen at the end in fluorescent yellow jackets and as you walk past, one of them wishes you luck. The stadium is packed to capacity and it roars at you as you emerge into the weak evening sunshine, and although you and your opposite number have come out together, you know it's not the Revolyutsiya coach who is being cheered. Your own dedicated Hardwick supporters outnumber the visitors by at least twenty to one tonight, and you can feel their expectancy rippling around the familiar ground. You raise your hand at all four walls of fans in appreciation, knowing how much their noise settles and boosts your players every time.

You pat each member of your team on the back, giving words of encouragement to them as they file past you and on to the pitch. Now turn the page to find out what you're up against tonight . . .

Revolyutsiya Apelsyn

Manager: Ivan Karamatsov

Formation:	4-3-3
Defence Skill:	16
Midfield Skill:	18
Attack Skill:	18

Copy these opposition Skill values into the boxes on Match Sheet 1 (page 274). You should now be able to see how your Defence compares with their Attack, and so on.

You're ready to kick off! Turn to 460.

206

So Homens da Guerra, Liblonec Vyoslav and Lazzaro di Savena join Hardwick City in the draw for the semi-finals, which is due to take place tomorrow morning at eleven. Hardly time to draw breath is there? Head home and turn to 338 when you've had a good night's sleep . . . unless there's something you want to investigate first, in which case turn to 210.

207

Score 1 point for this answer. You'll need to tot these up later, so make a note somewhere on your Fact Sheet (page 284). Now turn to 128.

208

You summon Charlotte-Ann to you as a matter of urgency, and quickly explain the situation. She nods, and begins to arrange a series of crystals in what appears to be a 4-3-3 formation. She unpacks her Tarot cards, dealing them slowly and precisely while she murmurs to herself. Finally, she removes from a piece of purple velvet a bright brass pendulum, which she swings over the entire arrangement. And almost immediately, you notice that it's having absolutely no effect whatsoever. What an almighty load of hokum! But what did you expect? Get back to the real world and return to the paragraph you just came from.

209

Have you selected your two Qualities yet? If so, turn to 410. If not, make your next choice from the list below.

Tactical	(Turn to 518)
Diplomatic	(Turn to 503)
Assertive	(Turn to 397)
Flexible	(Turn to 479)
Inspirational	(Turn to 455)
Instinctive	(Turn to 247)

210

If you've heard something about a device, you should have a note of two letters followed by a number. Add this number to this paragraph and go there now. Otherwise stop speculating and go home (turn to 338).

211

You greet your team in the dressing room. You are aware that for most of them this represents a pinnacle in their careers, and the determination on their faces as they gather round you tells you how much setting up a home advantage tonight would mean to them.

'You've all shown me what you can do in rehearsals,' you tell them, 'but the group stage is over. This is opening night on the main stage and I want to see cats out there tonight, not les miserables.'

'*Me-zay-ra-bluh*,' Duval corrects grumpily, but the point is made and you usher the players out in the direction of Hardwick's adoring thousands.

Check the stats of your opposition by turning to 28 if you're playing Real Sabadell, 476 if you're playing Noordenhaarenijk, or 108 if you're playing Cochons d'Inde.

212

The dogs either see you or smell you, and it's too late. The branches of the trees are too high to climb, and you are dragged down by hungry Alsatians before you can even cry out. You really, really don't want to know what happens next.

Turn to 101.

213

Monday arrives, thankfully without injury or incident. You and your squad begin your journey to the away leg of your semi-final, and you are all brimming with anticipation as you board the plane. But where is your destination?

The Czech Republic?   (Turn to 56)

Italy?   (Turn to 230)

214

'Nigel's right,' you say, turning to Heather. 'We can't go on playing this game. Let's get it all out in the open. I'll arrange a meeting with Steve Fitzgerald first thing.'

Heather protests, but you've made up your mind.

Have you?

If you're having second thoughts, agree with Heather by turning to 447. Otherwise stick to your plan, get a good night's rest and meet Steve in the morning: turn to 261.

215

Are Danny Knox and Jamie Coates both playing? If so, turn to 18. If not, turn to 382.

216

Roll one dice. If you roll 1 or 2, turn to 180. If you roll 3 or 4, turn to 325. If you roll 5 or 6, turn to 533.

217

And so your story ends. Three suspended players, a European Cup campaign cut short at the quarter-finals, and a new season to think about. The players look dejected, but you have to tell them to be proud of their achievements this year. And that there's a new challenge waiting for them all next time. And to keep doing what they do best for Hardwick City. And so on.

Turn to 101.

218

As your aeroplane climbs steeply into the night sky and Germany recedes invisibly below you, you sip an iced drink and consider your situation. Yes, Hardwick still have every chance of progressing in this competition, and considering the sudden loss of three talented players that's nothing short of a miracle.

But in the pit of your stomach there is a nagging feeling, and you can't relax. Is this it? Your players took steroids, got caught, and now the team and the fans all have to suffer the consequences. Or is there more to it? And even if there is, what can you possibly do?

You can't help feeling rather alone as your journey takes you back to your country, your town, your club and your office.

Hold on. What's this waiting for you on your desk? Turn to 159.

219

Here is the result of tonight's other semi-final (first leg scores in brackets).

Homens da Guerra 2(1) v Lazzaro di Savena 0(2)
Homens da Guerra win 3 − 2 on aggregate

Turn to 22.

220

The man in the article plays as a centre-forward. Because of his injury, your opponents will have to play with a new attacking formation, which they are not as comfortable with. For tomorrow's match, you may subtract **2** from their Attack Skill.

When the plane touches down, turn to 355.

221

The corner of one page is turned down. You open the catalogue there, and you see that the page is crammed with advertisements for bodybuilding supplements: amino acids, testosterone compounds and weight gain pills, all available for mail order with product codes and prices. Someone has ringed one of the codes in black biro – a product called Hexabulin.

Where is this getting you? 'Doctor Orders Pills' wouldn't exactly make the headlines. Do you want to look up Hexabulin on the Internet (turn to 381), close the drawer and try the filing cabinets (turn to 23), or turn off the light and leave (turn to 320)?

222

Looking around, it seems that the only thing heavy enough to use is the chair. This is going to make one hell of a racket. If you still want to go ahead with your wanton destruction, turn to 72. If you decide to search through the desk drawers instead, turn to 491. If you leave the room quietly, turn to 320.

223

Your scheme is spot on. Your players will benefit from your expertise even better than you'd hoped, and this will give you special advantages in the next **two** matches only. You now have **5** points which you may divide as you wish between your Midfield Skill and your Attack Skill. For example, you may wish to add 3 to your Attack and 2 to your Midfield. Note that this does not permanently increase the skill of any of your players.

Make a note of that on your next two Match Sheets and turn to 278.

224

The other players are kidding with Jamie about the rivalry between him and his opposite number, Ray Richards. He is grinning, safe in the knowledge that he is highly thought-of in your squad, and quietly enjoying being the centre of attention. But he knows the England manager will be watching both keepers tonight from somewhere in the stands, and Jamie is desperate to put in a great performance. Add **1** to Jamie's Skill for this match only; make a note of this on Match Sheet 2.

Turn to 307.

225

The two leave together and you are alone in your office. There is so little time between the quarters and the semis that you decide it would be counter-productive to embark on a new training plan. You instruct your coaching assistants to put the team through a light fitness schedule with dribbling and teamwork exercises.

Since you have a mole in your midst, it is more important than ever to stick together as a team. You know Steve will be doing his best to fit into the team as though everything's normal, and as long as he keeps thinking you're ignorant of his plotting you still have an advantage.

Turn to 213.

226

What an awesome result! This was potentially your hardest match in the group, and you've come away with three massive points. The Bayern players look stunned: they've been taught a lesson in football tonight.

When you've enjoyed your giant-killing glory, there's a nice fresh table waiting to be filled in. Turn to 89.

227

Notes are made and heads nodded – the hacks seem satisfied with your response.

Turn to 326.

228

This is your chance to fire up your team with a few choice words. What would be appropriate?

Lavish praise? (Turn to 96)

A short talk to lift their mood with constructive criticism and advice drawn from your own experience? (Turn to 12)

An absolute roasting? (Turn to 371)

229

You grab at the metal handle and push. The door doesn't even budge. You shake the door, screaming, but the caretaker has wandered off and doesn't hear a thing.

You lose your strength, fall backwards and die in this horrible place. Turn to 101.

230

This is what the experts are saying about Lazzaro di Savena.

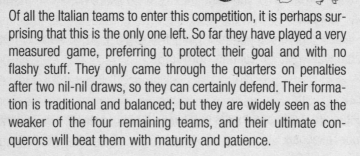

TEAM PROFILE
Lazzaro di Savena
Italy

Of all the Italian teams to enter this competition, it is perhaps surprising that this is the only one left. So far they have played a very measured game, preferring to protect their goal and with no flashy stuff. They only came through the quarters on penalties after two nil-nil draws, so they can certainly defend. Their formation is traditional and balanced; but they are widely seen as the weaker of the four remaining teams, and their ultimate conquerors will beat them with maturity and patience.

Star Player: Mirko Venturi
Central Midfielder

In a recent TV interview with Italy's Mediaset station, Mirko Venturi claimed to have a girlfriend in every European capital city – 'so I never get lonely when I travel,' he said, looking into the camera and raising one eyebrow. When he's not making

MIRKO VENTURI

men jealous by flirting with their girlfriends, he's making them jealous by showing his prowess on the pitch. His role is officially a central one, but he is talented and confident enough to make forays deep into enemy territory. His strike rate has dropped in recent times however, and some are saying he's had his day. Perhaps they're right. Or perhaps they're just . . . jealous?

Select your own team now. When you've done that, turn to 118.

231

Nigel Douglas turns to you as soon as the announcement is made.

'What are our chances?'

'As good as any,' you suggest. 'It's a pressure situation, playing two away matches on the hoof, but if we can keep their attackers frustrated for ninety minutes they'll feel more scared coming to us.'

'And what about the other pressures?' he asks in a lower voice.

You look around. It's too risky talking about it here. You indicate the door with your eyes and the two of you get up to leave the room while the players and staff talk excitedly about the fixture in three days' time. As you leave, you catch sight of Heather McCullough who is standing at the back, silently chewing gum. She gives you a barely perceptible nod.

Turn to 429.

232

Here are the opposition's stats this time round. You will notice that they are stronger this time, because they have the home advantage. Copy the details on to your Match Sheet in the usual way. (Perhaps you've heard of an injury to one of their squad? If so, you'll remember to deduct some Skill points.) When you are ready, turn to 404.

Noordenhaarenijk

Manager: Dirck Groot
Formation: 4-4-2
Defence Skill: 19
Midfield Skill: 24
Attack Skill: 22

233

'There are two types of people in this game,' you tell your assembled squad, holding up two fingers to prove it. 'Winners, and losers.'

You raise an eyebrow to see if anyone can think of any other type of person. They can't, and you continue.

'Some say enjoy your football. Some say try your best, and if you lose, at least you tried. I say you can't take that to the bank. There's no prize for pluckiness in this job, and I'm only interested in one result tonight. This is their home, and they'll be looking to score; but I want that manager feeling he can't get a goal for hide nor hair. Now get out there and bang some in.'

Sheer poetry. Your booming conviction has them all pumped up and ready to go. Add **1** to your Attack Skill for this match only, and a further 1 if you have the Assertive or Inspirational quality.

When you're ready to kick off, turn to 336.

234

'It's best if I do it,' you say. 'If anyone sees Heather hanging around the players' area it might look suspicious.'

The two of them agree, and you bid each other good night before making your way downstairs to the empty dressing room. You pull at the door to Steve's locker, and it opens. No surprise; it's mostly bare, but stuck to the inside of the door is a postcard with a picture of a church on the front. You pull it away from the door and read. And it's the oddest card you've ever seen, because there are no words. Just this:

Does that help you with anything else you've found so far? Either way, you should probably copy this down on your Fact Sheet (or make a note of this paragraph to refer to later).

Turn to 114

235

Paul Price will turn out to be a liability. He's the youngest in your squad by far and is a real prima donna, always looking for ways to impress you. That might be all right on the training field, but not at this level of competition. Price has a new Skill of just **3**, and you must also lose **1** Morale for your poor decision.

Make these changes and turn to 516.

236

You return to your office and find that Nigel Douglas has been looking for you. Nigel is your new club chairman, and the club is a much happier place since he took over from Victor — his selfish, useless predecessor. There's a note on your door from him asking to see you. Better not keep the boss waiting. Turn to 62.

237

How do you want to reply to this question?

'Their talents will be missed, but I still have lots of tricks up my sleeve.' (Turn to 501)

'I've hardly noticed they've gone.' (Turn to 423)

238

If you've finished with the contents of the parcel, turn to 186. Otherwise you may now open the small box (turn to 464), the bigger box (turn to 162), or read the card (turn to 116).

239

You're on your way! An away win is worth its weight in gold, and your opponents will have all the work to do when they come to you on Friday. Carry the score over to your next Match Sheet and turn to 324.

240

You look everywhere – in the plant pots, under the telephone, behind the books in the bookcase. And then you find it. Tucked under the rim of your desk – nestled in a wad of *chewing gum* of all things! – is a tiny black microphone. It's not one of the ones Higson supplied to you; you already know where those two are. And yet they're the only way your voice could find its way to your own recorder.

Think, think . . .

If you haven't listened to the whole of the tape yet, turn to 148 to do so. Otherwise turn to 441.

241

For the first time in this competition, you're going to have to play extra time. That's an extra thirty minutes of football, and you've only got five minutes to recover before it starts.

Your players have put everything they've got into the first ninety minutes, and there's a chance any one of them could be worn out from the sheer exertion of the match so far. For each player on your team, roll two dice. If you roll 2 or 12, that player is exhausted. You may substitute them within the normal rules of the game; if you don't, each exhausted player must lose 1 point of Skill for the first 15 minutes and a further point for the second 15 minutes.

Of course if you wish to make any other substitutions you may do that too. But remember that if no goals are scored in extra time, a penalty shoot-out will take place; and you'll need your best spot-kickers for that.

Do you have the Inspirational managerial quality? If you do, remember this gives you special bonuses in extra time (turn to 455 for a reminder).

When you've finished making necessary amendments to your team, send them back into the lion's den for more. Play just two 15-minute segments. Then turn to 262.

242

You call Eddie up on his mobile, and explain the choices you've made.

'I've only got one problem with that,' he says after a few seconds' consideration. 'I know lads like Paul Price, and although he's a goal scorer, he's just a boy. He'll need more moulding before he's ready for this level of competition.'

You still can't help worrying that the team would be too thin up front without him.

'Who do you suggest then?' you ask impatiently.

'I've had half an eye on Roberto Zapatero for a few months now,' Eddie tells you. He sees the surprise in your face. 'I know he's usually played over on the right midfield, but he's got natural ability in front of goal and he's always racing up there whenever he can. Good vision, right place right time – that sort of thing.'

You think about this.

'And he's banged in a few,' Eddie adds helpfully.

Well? Are you going to stick with your original plan and draft Paul Price into your squad? If so, turn to 235. If you'd rather go with Eddie's advice, turn to 81.

243

Back on the pitch, the referee looks from one side to the other. When he's satisfied that both teams are in position, he blows his whistle to start the second half.

Play it out as before and turn to 315 when the game is over.

244

Was it a scoring draw (turn to 290)? Or was it nil-nil (turn to 196)?

245

The club's own modestly slender list of VIPs, past and present, sits on your shelf where it has gathered dust since you arrived at the club some years ago. Apart from people looking up their own names for a thrill, you'd always wondered who read books like this.

You take it down, flicking through the pages while you make your way back to your seat.

'Ventner, Gregory,' you read aloud, setting the book down in front of your companions. The three of you continue to read in silence.

Born August 15, 1973. Transferred to Hardwick from Calverton FC aged 19.

'Calverton – that was on the address as well!' you exclaim.

Shares a mother with Steven Fitzgerald, age 16, currently with Hardwick's youth team. We expect these two young talents to have a massive impact on this club's future!

Underneath the text is a black-and-white copy of a photograph, showing two boys with their arms round each other's shoulder and wearing the old club strip.

That's all. But it's enough, and the three of you look at one another.

'Half-brothers,' Nigel says. 'I had no idea.'

'And they both used to play for Hardwick,' Heather says.

One of them still does, you think to yourself.

If you haven't already, see whether the Internet throws up any more information by turning to 519. If you'd rather look up the name in the phone book, turn to 112. If you've finished your research, turn to 542.

246

Take the penalty in the normal way (refer to page 25 if you want a reminder). If you score, remember to mark the goal on your Match Sheet (like you'd forget). Then turn to 304.

247

Your heart rules your head, and you go with your gut feeling. In your opinion, that's how you've got to the top of the football tree: by doing first and thinking later, if at all. This gets you a certain respect from the people who see how passionate about the game you are. But it also means you lose your cool head sometimes, which can land you in trouble. You'll receive special instructions later in the book about all that.

For now, just write 'Instinctive' under Manager Qualities on your Fact Sheet (page 284).

Important: being Instinctive means you may not choose the quality Tactical.

Now turn to 209.

248

The fax contains details of the transfer market. You may take this opportunity to buy new players if you think you have enough money. You may also think about selling some of your own players if you wish. What are you interested in doing first?

Buying?   (Turn to 126)
Selling?   (Turn to 468)

If neither, or you've finished here, turn to 170.

249

The players were looking forward to having a mini-celebration with their boss, and when you don't turn up they are disappointed. Lose **2** Morale and turn to 511.

250

There are a number of players available for purchase at the moment. You may, of course, use your existing budget of 10 million pounds to try to buy some of them. Alternatively, you might want to sell one or two of your own players to bump up your budget even more. What do you want to do first?

Have a look at who is for sale? (Turn to 350)

Think about selling a player of your own? (Turn to 314)

Stop doing business and get on with preparations for the next match? (Turn to 521)

251
Turn to 298.

252
Your budget stands at 10 million pounds, which would be healthy enough if it weren't for your sudden shortage of players. But there's a spare hundred thousand in the kitty set aside for new staff, and for that money you should be able to get some-one useful to accompany the team for the remainder of the competition.

You fires 'em, and you hires 'em. Who would benefit the club?

A head talent scout? (Turn to 316)

A goalkeeping coach? (Turn to 352)

A physiotherapist? (Turn to 515)

An interpreter? (Turn to 127)

A psychic? (Turn to 522)

Remember you can only hire one individual! If you'd rather go it alone, turn to 525.

253
You watch as the door behind Greg opens, and Heather enters the room. She winks at you and holds her finger to her lips. Your heart swells as you watch her creep up behind Ventner, and you wait for

the moment as she clubs him over the head or whatever she's going to do to save you . . .

Instead she covers his eyes with her hands.

'Guess who?' she says.

Greg smiles broadly.

'Darling,' he says, keeping his gun pointed straight at you. 'You came.'

'I had an escort,' she says, kissing Greg on the cheek and turning to look at you.

Turn to 173.

254

Friday 7th – Match Day 5

Tonight's matches are crucial. At 7:45 there will still be eight teams in this competition; by 10:15 there will only be four.

It's the away leg of your quarter-final, and that means two things. First, you are at a disadvantage. Away matches are always harder, and that counts double for European games. But second, any goals you score tonight are crucial, and your opponents will be desperate to keep a clean sheet.

Remember, tonight's result will be added to your first leg result to get an aggregate total: and only the overall winner will progress to the semis.

It's time to pick your team. Turn to 394.

255

You dash out of Dr McCullough's office, not wanting to waste another moment in the stuffy basement. You take the stairs three at a time and lock your office door behind you. It was only six hours ago that you set up the listening device, so your heart leaps as you pull open your desk drawer and see that the tape is wound on by over two-thirds. You must have caught her having a conversation! You click rewind, but during the time it takes for the cassette to whirr back to its starting position you realise that the microphone could have been activated when you confronted her this morning. Do you listen to the tape anyway (turn to 75), or think of something else to do (turn to 181)?

256

The players stare at the floor. Your rant has shocked them into silence. Turn to 236.

257

You freeze, completely trapped, and seconds last for minutes as the two of you lock eyes across the aisle. The dull roar of the engines fills your head.

'Erm . . . I was just – going to –' you bluster.

'Don't you know you can't use phones on airplanes?' Steve tells you. 'You'd better turn that off before she sees it.'

He indicates the flight attendant who is still serving coffee a few seats in front of you.

You feel like an express train just passed within an inch of your nose.

'Hey, nice phone, boss. I got that one,' he adds sleepily as his eyes close, and he once again falls into the slow, heavy breathing of one who is deeply asleep.

A close, close call. Breathe out again and turn to 425.

258

There is a stack of junk mail, including a letter telling you that you have been randomly selected by computer to win a cash prize!! Next to it is a sealed cardboard parcel, posted Special Delivery and covered with 'Fragile' stickers.

What do you want to open first? The letter (turn to 459) or the parcel (turn to 200)? If you'd rather ignore them both, turn to 320.

259

You leave your office and go down one flight of stairs to the basement. This is where the surgery and the sick bay are located, as well as the medicine store and doctor's office. The medical facilities here have been overhauled this season and the whole floor gleams with chrome and polished glass.

You make your way to Heather's door and read the brass plate: H. McCullough, M.D. You knock, but of course there's no answer: it's been a long day and it's already nearly midnight. You may try the handle if you wish (turn to 151), or wait until morning (turn to 320).

260

Lucky, lucky. One for the card – it's not red – and one for the fact the ref isn't pointing to the spot, so it's not a penalty either.

First, roll a dice for each of your defenders in turn. Keep going until you roll a 1; that player has been booked, so make a note of this next to his name on your Match Sheet. Next, you have a dangerous free kick to defend. Take this for the opposition in the usual way. Remember to update your Match Sheet if they score.

Was that a sigh of relief or a sigh of despair? Either way, you should now turn to 382.

261

It's nine o'clock the following morning. You, Heather and Nigel are gathered in your office. Steve Fitzgerald is under instructions to come to your office first thing, and after a few minutes there is a knock at the door.

Steve enters, and looks immediately taken aback when he sees all three of you sitting there. But when he recovers himself, you are more shocked by what he says next.

'I resign. Immediately.'

'Steve – what? But –'

He doesn't let you finish.

'I took the steroids. It was my choice. Stupid me,' he says mechanically, almost as if he's rehearsed it. 'No further comment until I speak to my lawyer.'

He is out the door and down the stairs before any of you can think of what to say.

You've blown it. Steve has closed up like a clam, and there's nowhere left to go.

After all, he hasn't actually done anything *illegal*.

Has he?

Turn to 101.

262

What was the score in extra time?

If you won, turn to 372. If you lost, turn to 217. If you drew, turn to 281.

263

The player concerned is a left-back. Hs injury means your opposition's defence is depleted, especially against right-footed players, and you may deduct **2** from the Defence Skill of your opponents during tomorrow's game.

Make a note of that and turn to 355 when you arrive.

264

Turn to 526.

265

Zaki only needs to glance at the touch judge to see that the flag is . . . down. The goal stands and the striker wheels away, arms out like an aeroplane, before throwing himself on to the ground belly first. He skids like this along the wet grass, coming to a stop in front of an adoring visitors' stand. You see him look up at the fans with a big grin, but only for a moment as the rest of your team jump on top of him and he disappears under a pile of delighted Hardwick players.

Ah, just like the old days. You can get booked for being that happy these days; he was lucky. The ref spots the ball and blows the whistle for the restart, but time's up; turn to 402.

266

The golden goal rule went out years ago, but you wouldn't know it. The friendly half of the crowd stop chewing their knuckles and erupt in furious celebration. They don't stop even when the referee respots the ball and play continues. But the Portuguese team is spent and Hardwick just have to hang on. Every soft pass gets a cheer, and Hardwick hardly give up possession. The seconds tick away, desperately slowly, until the whistle goes for the last time today.

You run out on to the pitch, coat billowing, hardly believing what's happened. Fireworks are spraying out Hardwick's colours into the sky, and your players come streaming from all directions towards you. You are hoisted on to the shoulders of Jamie Coates and Danny Knox, and time stops as you hear your name boomed out by thousands of fans in their appreciation of your achievement: the greatest in Hardwick's history. Turn to 547.

267

You held them to a draw, and that's the main thing. But failing to score means the pressure is on you to keep a clean sheet when they play you at home on Friday, as any goals they score could count double. Better make sure your goalie's on top form.

Turn to 324.

268

The postmark is identical to the one on the back of the postcard that was in Steve's locker – the one with the strange alphabet on the back. You also recognise that the address on the front is Steve's own, and he has just crossed it out and reused the envelope. Do you want to look more closely at the address (turn to 95), read the fax (turn to 248), or leave for the night (turn to 527)?

269

Of course! That's it!

All three players took a vitamin supplement – one that could have been contaminated with something, at the factory perhaps, or maybe there was a mix-up in the delivery, or the packing. Your mind is racing. You can clear the players' names now and –

Wait.

No, that's stupid. Of course there hasn't been a mix-up. Your own team doctor, Heather McCullough, makes these vitamin supplements up herself according to each player's needs. Every single chemical that passes a player's lips gets checked and double-checked by Dr McCullough personally, and as far as you know she's never made a mistake in her life.

So what's going on? If you still think the vitamin theory is worth checking out – it's the only one you've got, after all – turn to 297. If not, and you think the players are guilty as hell and just pulling the wool over your eyes, turn to 68.

270

Thursday 20th – 2 days to the final

Another day passes and you are a day closer to the final.

If you have got this far, you must have discovered an address. With so little time remaining, now could be your only chance to investigate it. If you do, turn to 146. If you don't, turn to 377.

271

You sit at your desk, and study the details of the first part of the European League Cup Competition. Here's a reminder of how it works. There are three other teams in your group. That means you have to play three matches, and the two teams with the most points go through to the next round. Win all your matches and you're sure to qualify!

There are four groups altogether, and you were drawn in Group B. Take a good long look. Isn't there something beautiful and pure about a blank table, brimming with expectation, open to a million possible futures?

Group B	Played	W	D	L	Points
Kott Fotbollar (Swe)	0				0
Hardwick City (Eng)	0		·		0
Bayern Badetuch (Ger)	0				0
Revolyutsiya Apelsyn (Ukr)	0				0

Fixtures:

Wednesday 15th :	Kött Fotbollar v Bayern Badetuch
	Hardwick City v Revolyutsiya Apelsyn
Tuesday 21st :	Bayern Badetuch v Hardwick City
	Revolyutsiya Apelsyn v Kött Fotbollar
Wednesday 29th :	Hardwick City v Kött Fotbollar
	Revolyutsiya Apelsyn v Bayern Badetuch

It's not the easiest group in the competition. Kött Fotbollar are reckoned to be the best team in the Swedish national league, and German side Bayern Badetuch have a solid reputation in this competition. But it could be worse. Revolyutsiya Apelsyn, from Ukraine, are relative minnows in the European League Cup. They will be your first opposition, and Hardwick are firm favourites to see them off.

It's Monday, and that match kicks off at 7:45 p.m. on Wednesday. If you want to study Revolyutsiya's credentials, turn to 388. If not, you should go and meet with your team to prepare them for the match – turn to 351.

272

If you're here with Nigel, turn to 163. If Heather, turn to 253.

273

The phone rings and rings, and you are about to hang up when a gruff voice answers.

'Higson.'

Same old Higson, answering just as if he were on duty.

You introduce yourself and hope that he remembers you.

'Of course I remember,' he tells you in that voice which always sounds cross and impatient but behind which there is a thoughtful and gentle man. 'Is anything the matter? You sound worried.'

You explain the situation, your interviews with the three players and your hunch about the vitamin supplements.

'Sounds like you haven't got a lot,' he tells you. 'If you plonked this on my desk I'd tell you to sod off and come back when you've got some facts. Have you even talked to the doctor yet?'

You confess that you haven't.

'I would, if I were you. Which I'm quite glad I'm not,' he adds.

You thank him and you are about to say goodbye, when he speaks again.

'Listen – I have to admit, I'm a bit bored since I retired. Not much to do except potter round in the garden. Keep in touch, won't you? Ring me again next time you've got something you want to discuss.'

You promise you will. Make a careful note of his number on your Fact Sheet: it's 0787 911999.

Now turn to 422.

274

Your announcement that you are treating all your players to a slap-up feed at their favourite trattoria is roundly greeted by the squad. It won't be the same without Salvatore Duce deciding what everyone will eat and chatting up the waitresses (who are usually English and can't understand a word he's saying). But you decide the team has richly deserved a treat.

And you reflect on the careers of the Hardwick Three, and how they hang in the balance. You'd always set yourself up as not only the manager of the team, but the guardian of each of the players as well. Now you know about the plot to bring down the club you feel determined to put your own future on the line for the three innocent players. If you are to uncover the plot against Hardwick, now is the time.

But how do you intend to get to Greg Ventner? The thought troubles you all the way to the restaurant, and when you see Steve Fitzgerald laughing and joking with one of the other players it cuts into you like a knife.

Turn to 169.

275

As your plane lands you safely back home, you take some time to consider Hardwick's situation. You told your players that they had nothing to fear, but you know that's not true. Now Hardwick are through to the semis, whoever is trying to bring down the club will surely redouble their efforts to get you knocked out of this competition. And working for them, from right inside the club, is your very own Steve Fitzgerald. Who is sitting three feet to your right. Snoring. With his mobile phone poking out of his shirt pocket.

Casting a quick eye around the plane you realise that most people have fallen asleep after dinner. The lights are already dimmed, the flight attendant has her back to you, and this could be your best chance for information. Do you dare?

If you risk a stealth raid on Steve's top pocket, turn to 520.

If you'd rather not chance it, turn to 191.

276

Here's how it works. To see how much you can get for your goalkeeper, roll one dice and subtract it from Rob Rose's Skill. This is the number of millions that are being offered. If you accept the offer, cross Rob's name off your Squad Details on page 285 and add the money on to your Budget. Of course, you may refuse the offer, but a better one isn't going to come along!

When you've finished, go back to 250.

277

You are relieved as you tread on the next tile and it takes your weight. There is still absolute silence. You may now choose from the following tiles in front of you: the ball (turn to 166), the whistle (turn to 174), or the boot (turn to 448).

278

Tuesday 4th – Match Day 4
Once again, the day is upon you when you will be called on to pour all your managerial talents into your team to make sure they come

out with a result. But this time, the stakes are higher than you have ever experienced in your career. Two legs of ninety minutes against one of the best teams on the continent, the first to be held at Hardwick's home ground tonight. Despite the thousands of column inches written about fixtures like this, it's really quite simple: you're at home, so you need to win. Nil-nil is the next best result, because keeping out the away goals is so important. Anything else will be seen as disappointing.

Take some time to familiarise yourself with the opposition. Who are they?

Real Sabadell?   (Turn to 395)
Noordenhaarenijk?   (Turn to 489)
Cochons d'Inde?   (Turn to 393)

279

Before you can reach the ladder, the door to the incinerator swings open above your head and a heavy box of papers is thrown in. It hits you square in the forehead and you reel backwards, tripping over a black sack and landing spread-eagled in a particularly foul-smelling pool of gunk. You are winded and dizzy from the blow to your head, and for a while your head swims. At first you are only aware of the dank, rotting stench of rubbish which seeps all around you. But then another smell replaces it, sweet and pleasant, and you feel sleepy . . . and in the distant darkness above you there is a light, getting bigger, closer . . . closer . . .

ffffffffffUMP. There is a flash, and your thoughts suddenly come together. The smell is paraffin. The light was a match. Flames are licking hungrily at the black walls now, forcing clouds of filthy smoke and sparks up the narrow chimney high above you. Fumes fill your nose, your eyes are streaming; a wall of heat pushes against you, forcing you back until you are sitting upright against the back wall of the incinerator.

Spiders and woodlice scuttle out of cracks in the concrete wall to make a break for it.

The caretaker must have thrown the box in and he didn't even look inside. Why would he?

No one knows you are here.

Did you bring anything with you? It wasn't a fire-extinguisher by any chance, was it? If it was, turn to 504. If it wasn't, or you brought nothing, turn to 493.

280

Did you speak with all three players? If so, turn to 446. If not, turn to 68.

281

If neither team scored in extra time, turn to 119. If both teams scored, turn to 482.

282

You draw up a training plan for the week ahead, paying particular attention to containment at the back and fine-tuning the offside trap. You may add **1** to your Defence score for the next match only. Turn to 102.

283

Nigel strides over to the tiled area, thinks for a moment, then takes a stride forward. You follow in his footsteps. Roll two dice. If you roll double six, turn to 442. If you roll anything else, turn to 434.

284

Which flight do you choose?

The left one?	(Turn to 251)
The middle one?	(Turn to 298)
The right one?	(Turn to 367)

285

It's late in the match and, as expected, the Spanish midfield are starting to wilt. Hardwick's time in possession is creeping up and up, and the pressure is building in the midfield like a volcano about to erupt.

There is a sudden swell of momentum from your team, and it's a bit like watching the tide wash over a beach. Klaus Wehnert receives the ball from a long pass and begins a run up field. In a spectacular display of Route One football he thunders up the centre of the pitch, spraying weaker opposition players before him like driftwood. Real Sabadell are being forced back in numbers beneath the weight of the Hardwick attack. You see that Ian Leslie has cleverly dropped back just a little into a centre forward's role and is matching the German giant stride for stride, twenty yards ahead. With an unselfish precision typical of your mature midfielder, Klaus splits the marooned defence in two with a tidy side-footed pass. Ian Leslie hardly breaks stride as he collects the ball to finish the job. The keeper comes out to meet him; for a split second Ian pretends to hesitate, then darts right to round the keeper and slots the ball into the open goal.

The whole move was built on the confidence of your team to impose their superior midfield firepower, and you're the architect of that. Chalk up the goal on your Match Sheet and continue the match. When the final whistle is blown, turn to 384.

286

Football is a fickle game. Only fifteen minutes ago you were clear favourites, and now you're the wrong end of two-one. But you urge your players to play tight, attacking football, and you make a substitution that you will later think was one of the defining tactical decisions of your career. Duval is fast and clever, but against a depleted side you need depth, not speed. Hoggart is a superior passer of the ball, and better able to draw off defenders. You make the swap and the players return to the field.

It works. After ten minutes of cat-and-mouse football John Hoggart centres a ball at the feet of Bostock, who plays it right back to him on the wing. He controls it with his left, looks up to take in the arrangement of players, and immediately picks out Stevens on the far side of goal with his right. Stevens chests the ball down and strokes it to Ben Parker who is standing his ground near the spot. He lashes a clean strike into the top of the goal, so powerful it nearly slices the net from its rigging. The game is even again on sixty minutes, and surely now Hardwick have the advantage. But Homens da Guerra have decided to play a dampening game, and spend the next half hour hanging on to the draw and trying to tire your players out. The game is a psychological one now. Hardwick's attacks are thwarted each time, and although all the action is in the Guerra half your players can't create a real scoring chance. Ninety minutes ticks around and it's two-all.

Two whole periods of extra time to play, and the break is mercilessly short. But you know your players are at the peak of their ability, and you are on the lookout for anyone who is flagging. You send them into the ring for another bout.

The first fifteen minutes are a typically nervy affair with several players being ruled offside from mistimed runs and some twitchy defending from both sides. The second period is different though. Homens da Guerra know they are down to ten men, and their tiring team is feeling the pinch of that missing player. It's clear from their slow game and lone striker that they're just playing the time out, hoping for penalties. By comparison Hardwick look focussed and calm. Maybe it's something to do with being at full strength again, or maybe that last equaliser made them feel they were fated to be in this cup; either way it's working.

Hardwick are pushing forward and making the most of the width of the pitch, and John Hoggart again makes space for himself on the right touchline just inside your half. He lines up a cross before side-footing the ball into the stride of Will Frost. Frost rushes one defender, who seems terrified of putting in a tackle so close to full-time, and takes the ball past him before whipping a cross into the eighteen-yard area. It's one of those balls that dips more quickly than you're expecting, but Ben Parker knows exactly where it's going and he doesn't even wait for it to bounce. Pivoting perfectly on his left foot like Rudolf Nureyev, he takes the ball on the top of his right boot and with laser-guided precision tucks it into the top left corner of the net. The goalkeeper looks like he's on sentry duty.

Turn to 266.

287

'It's all true. But I can't prove it,' you concede. Your blood runs cold as you realise you've been trapped.

Nigel Douglas explains to you coolly that you are in breach of your contract with the club, and that this gives him the right to suspend you pending a full investigation into your actions. He doesn't need to explain – you know you've had it. Turn to 101.

288

Bad luck. There are a lot of prints, but they're all overlapping and there isn't a single clear one. Ditch the knife and fork – unless you *really* want them as a souvenir – and turn to 408.

289

Mbaye looks unstoppable when he runs like this, darting and dum-mying his way towards goal. But Duval is marking him pace for pace, patiently refusing to give him a sight on goal. He can't stop him completely, but his quick reactions close down Mbaye's angle of attack, which allows de Carvalho to read the direction of the cross before it arrives. The ball comes floating in, but Carlos is per-fectly positioned and he climbs in the air to nod the ball powerfully away to safety.

An impressive attack has been turned into a display of clever and cooperative defending, and Carlos and Dmitri applaud each other. You and everyone else applaud them both. That's exactly what you're paying them for.

Play out the rest of the match as normal. When 90 minutes are up, turn to 384.

290

Away goals count double in these situations. Whoever was the away team in that match, therefore, goes above the other in the group. Let's hope it was you. Complete the table, then turn to 139.

291

Nigel Douglas rounds on her, his face full of anger.

'Give me one good reason why not,' he hisses, his hand still on the phone.

Heather's head and shoulders are slumped so that you can't see her face, and she is shaking and sobbing violently.

What do you do? If you think Nigel should go right ahead and inform the police, turn to 471. If you want to persuade him to wait while you question her yourselves, turn to 478.

292

It's only one point each, but away goals are valuable and could make all the difference when it comes to deciding who goes through to the next round. You should be pleased with that. Turn to 89 and record the result in the Group Table.

293

What do you say?

'The shame of being out of the cup is punishment enough. I hope to welcome them back to the club as soon as I can.'

(Turn to 449)

'The players' behaviour is being dealt with according to strict FA procedure.'   (Turn to 313)

294

Tuesday 21st – Match Day 2

Apart from Jamie Coates not knowing his *heiss* from his *kalt* and burning his head in the showers, everyone spends a peaceful night in the team hotel and arrives early for breakfast.

You are lucky that your players travel well. Internationally famous footballers are known for being delicate little flowers when they get too far away from home, and get upset very easily if the soup is too hot or the duvet isn't fluffy enough. But yours are far too busy eating and fooling around for that.

'What's this bread?' Rob Rose is saying. 'It's black!'

'Es ist *schwarzbrot*,' Klaus Wehnert tells him, tucking into a mountain of bread, jam, German sausage and boiled eggs. 'We have ze best breakfast in ze world.'

'Haven't they got choco pops?' Jed Stevens whines from the other table.

'*Haven't they got choccy pops?*' mocks Ant Bostock, and he throws a hard bread roll at Jed. It lands in his cup and splashes coffee all over him, making everyone laugh.

'Er – a bit more respect for our German hosts, please,' you say, throwing Jed a napkin. He swipes to catch it, misses, and knocks the rest of his coffee into his lap. There is uproar as everyone cracks up, including the waiting staff.

'And that's why you're not in goal,' you tell him.

Hold on – it's Match Day! There's serious stuff to do: finish your breakfast and turn to 7.

295

You explain everything over the phone. Greg Ventner and Steve Fitzgerald have risked everything to bring down Hardwick City. They have failed so far, and you have to expect them to try anything to destroy Hardwick's chances of winning the final. No one is safe.

'And that's why we can't afford to waste any more time,' you say a little breathlessly.

There is a pause while the information sinks in.

'Ok. Shall I meet you by your car?'

'Five minutes?' you suggest, feeling relieved not to be travelling alone.

Turn to 473.

296

You switch on your computer and the three of you gather round the screen. You type the name into your favourite search engine but with no result.

You've nothing to go on. You should try turning a few more

stones, as information has passed you by this time. And without information your campaign was always going to fail.

Turn to 101.

297

Deeper and deeper you go . . .

How are you intending to prove your little theory? – 'Hi Heather. I hope you don't mind if I perform a chemical analysis on everything you give the players from now on.' It's ridiculous. You've a football tournament to win, and you're not about to go all Famous Five. No, you think to yourself. Do this by the book, and there's bound to be a perfectly reasonable explanation.

This makes you feel like a TV detective. You dismiss the image with a shake of the head.

But it's given you an idea. Turn to 405.

298

You silently climb the stairs up to a door which opens on to a dingy second floor landing. The door swings shut behind you, however, and a single strip light flashes on automatically. There is a guard sitting in a chair at the end of the landing, and his eyes flick open at the same time as those of the three Alsatians who were sleeping at his feet.

They seem to be in rather a hurry to get to you. Turn to 101.

299

The whistle sounds and the match is underway. When the game reaches the 75th minute turn to 348.

CX-90. Somehow it doesn't sound pleasant; and whatever it is, it's in the locker room. You turn your car round and make your way over to the club, which has been closed up for the night. Your keys access all areas though, and you let yourself in to the main building and the locker room.

The strip lights flicker on and cast their artificial glare over the room. It's usually buzzing with activity here, but now its rows of steel lockers give it a morgue-like feeling. You take a deep breath and begin a systematic search of the place, starting on top of the lockers, behind the radiators, under the sinks . . .

Nothing.

You sit down on the large wooden bench in the centre of the room and begin wondering what to do if you can't find it. Could something have been hidden inside the shower heads, for example? Or behind the ceiling tiles? You hang your head and stare at the floor, picking at a splinter between the bench slats.

The bench . . . You get down on your hands and knees so you can see directly underneath where you've just been sitting, and there it is. An aluminium canister has been strapped with duck tape to the supporting column, right in the centre of the bench where no one would see it. Taped neatly to its side is a receiving device, and the two are linked by a thin white wire.

You remove the contraption from its binding and sit on the floor, turning it over in your hands. It's too small and light to be a bomb. But the electronics suggest some kind of detonator, and you don't want to try disarming it in case it's been wired against tampering.

CX-90 is printed in large menacing letters on the side of the canister. You tuck it in your pocket for later and leave the club for the night. Turn to 338.

301

You and Nigel haven't exchanged a word since you both came round, and you've only been dimly aware of his presence. He is on a chair to your left, and from his dishevelled appearance he must have spent the night unconscious like you. He looks frightened and is waiting for your lead.

'Quick,' you tell your chairman. 'Out the door, and don't breathe in until we're well out. Stick close behind me.'

He nods. Turn to 107.

302

You ring Bruce from your office, carefully spelling out the strange words to him.

'Never heard of anything like that in my life, mate,' he tells you. 'It's not a language, that's a fact. Some sort of code maybe, but you'll have to find a way to crack it.'

You thank him and hang up. Copy the strange words carefully on to your Fact Sheet and turn to 149.

303

Who did you just beat in the quarter-finals?

Real Sabadell?	(Turn to 144)
Cochons d'Inde?	(Turn to 392)
Noordenhaarenijk?	(Turn to 322)

304

Play out the match in the usual way. When it's all over, turn to 120.

305

You decide that your chosen attacker will receive the lion's share of your attention this week, with special focus on timing his runs correctly and receiving crosses. Roll two dice. If you roll doubles, turn to 49. If not, turn to 168.

306

Is Nigel with you? If so, turn to 301. If not, turn to 107.

307

'Welcome to Germany, where our own Hardwick City have come to see if they can topple the mighty Bayern Badetuch.'

'Let's hope so, John. Hardwick need to get out there and score a goal, because whoever scores first will definitely have the advantage.'

'These two teams have met twelve times in their history, chalking up six wins each and not a single draw. Can you believe that, Clive?'

'You never cease to amaze me, John.'

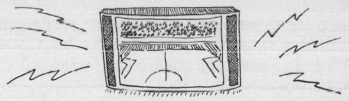

Gather your dice, and let the match begin. Remember, the rules are on page 22 if you need to refer to them. When 90 minutes are up, turn to 198.

308

You phone your secretary.

'Send Fitzgerald to my office urgently, please.'

You wonder how long you might have to wait for him to turn up, and you are a little surprised when there is a knock at your door in under a minute.

'Mornin', guv,' Steve says sunnily, putting his head inside the door. 'You wanted to see me?'

'The Storomere officials will be along in a bit, Steve. Any idea why?'

'Should I?'

There is a big friendly grin on his face, and for a moment you are lost for words. You expected something else – sullenness, guilt, something. Could you have made a mistake? No, the taped conversation said it all. He's bluffing. But what should you do? If you decide to confront him about everything you know, turn to 20. If you make up something else, turn to 544.

309

There is only one incinerator in the club, mostly used for burning rubbish left by the fans after a match. There hasn't even been a match since last week, so it's unlikely that the caretakers will have fired it up for a while . . .

You quietly open the door and step out into the corridor, trying for all you're worth to look completely normal. Staff are beginning to arrive to work now, and you hope no one can hear the frantic thudding of your heart.

You take the back exit out of the club main building and make your way across the rear car park. The incinerator is housed in a brick building next to the bins, and you duck round the back where you won't be seen.

There is a square metal door set into the brick at about waist height, and hanging off it is an open padlock. If you take the pad-lock with you, mark it on your Fact Sheet.

You swing open the door. Inside it's filthy. The walls are streaked with damp soot and the floor is covered with ash and rat droppings. It certainly hasn't been used in a while.

Strewn about the floor are several black rubbish sacks, and you have to climb down a short iron ladder to get to them. It's dirty work, but it doesn't take you long to find what you're looking for. Right at the back you see the boxes you were rooting through last night; there has been no attempt to hide them, but why should there be? Who in their right mind would be snooping around in here? All the evidence you need is in these boxes, and you've got Dr Dope's voice on tape in case there is any doubt.

Exhilarated and feeling like fate is back on your side, you begin making your way out of this hell-hole.

And then fate switches teams again. Turn to 279.

310

You instruct your secretary to summon the guilty players to the club as a matter of urgency. During the forty-five minutes it takes for them to arrive, you ponder the matter. You know that all three must have taken the banned supplement between the qualifier against Mazskaja and the Revolyutsiya match you just played; otherwise, the whole team would have been thrown out the competition. Three players, playing for an already successful team, all take the same illicit steroid at the same time. This is outrageous and unprece-dented, not to mention a bit odd.

All three are sitting nervously in the dressing room. Who do you want to speak to first?

Antek Bobak (Turn to 33)

Will Frost   (Turn to 24)
Salvatore Duce   (Turn to 152)

311
Turn to 434.

312
Did you select Paul Price? If so, turn to 99. Otherwise turn to 516.

313
Score 2 points for this answer. Make a note of this somewhere on your Fact Sheet (page 284) as you'll be told to add them up later. Now turn to 128.

314
There is interest from two other clubs in Rob Rose and Barry Voss. What do you want to do?

Consider selling Rob Rose?   (Turn to 276)
Consider selling Barry Voss?   (Turn to 532)
Neither of these, for now?   (Turn to 250)

315
Your first European match has ended. How did you do?
If you won, turn to 84.
If you drew, turn to 137.
If you lost, turn to 82.

316
You are able to hire Eddie Nimrod, an eagle-eyed talent spotter who has been in the game for nearly thirty years. He has worked

with the best British teams and calls himself 'The Hunter'. A good choice! If there are players out there who could fit into the Hardwick line-up, Eddie says he'll find them. He could be a valuable asset during this competition. Mark 'Eddie Nimrod, Chief Talent Scout' on your Fact Sheet on page 284, then turn to 480.

317

Wednesday 22nd, 7 a.m.

Your heart is pounding as you drive your sports car past security and park in your reserved space. You are here earlier than usual, so when you walk past the basement stairs on the way to your office you are not surprised to see that the lights are still off. That means Heather hasn't arrived yet.

It's only seven thirty, and she normally starts work at around eight. You have been worrying about your hidden microphone all night, and you are eager to see that it hasn't been dislodged by an over-eager cleaner. You descend the stairs, step into Dr McCullough's office and peer under her desk in the gloom. You had worried for nothing: it's still there, exactly where you placed it. What a relief!

Not for long. The door behind you is opening, and the lights have been turned on. Heather has arrived early. Turn to 444.

318

You turn off the phone again, reach over and slip it back into Steve's top pocket. This time he doesn't stir.

Turn to 191.

319

Your plan to sharpen team fitness and overall skill works like a charm. The players are committed and sure on the training pitch, recovery rates are high and they are reading each other better than ever. Add **2** to Fitness; and you now have **3** points which you may divide as you wish between your Defence, Midfield and Attack Skills for the next **two** matches only. For example, you may wish to add 2 to your Attack and 1 to your Defence. Note that this does not permanently increase the skill of any of your players.

Make a note of that on your next two Match Sheets and turn to 278.

320

It's late, and you're tired. You drive home and manage to catch a few vital hours of sleep. But it's back to work first thing in the morning – you've a football club to manage! Turn to 537.

321

Dinner utensils are strewn all over the table. Directly opposite you are the items Steve Fitzgerald was using.

You beckon over a friendly-looking waiter.

'I wondered,' you say, clearing your throat, 'if it might be possible to take a – souvenir – of a successful evening. It's a, erm, club tradition before a final.'

The waiter looks around and leans in close.

'*Si, si.* One condition,' the waiter replies. He taps his chest. 'Big fan. Can I have your autograph?'

You gladly oblige, signing his notebook.

'*Grazie mille,*' he says, admiring your signature. 'Now. What you like?'

You may take one item from the following:

Steve's wine glass

Steve's knife and fork
Steve's napkin

When you have made your decision, thank the waiter and turn to 328. Hey – don't forget to pay. You did remember your gold card, didn't you?

322

```
Homens da Guerra 2(1) v Cochons d'Inde 0(1)
Real Sabadell 1(2) v Liblonec Vyoslav 3(0)
Lazzaro di Savena 1(1) v Kött Fotbollar 0(1)
```

First leg scores are in brackets, so add them together to get the aggregate totals. When you have finished, turn to 206.

323

Having a set of prints is all well and good, but how can you use them to gain access to Ventner's house? Higson must have had something in mind when he sent you the kit, and you decide he is your only hope. You put the fingerprinted object in a polythene bag and write a brief note.

'Dear Higson,' you write, realising you still don't know his first name. 'These prints can get access to critical location. Can you help? One week left – URGENT.'

You sign off the note and seal the package. You clearly mark it 'Fragile' on both sides, copy Higson's home address on to the envelope and deposit the package into the mail.

Time to get some sleep – it's late, and you've a competition to win. Turn to 408.

324

Wednesday 12th, 8 a.m.

You sit in your office, busying yourself with paperwork to make sure your house is in order before resuming team training later this morning. The second leg of the semis is only two days away and you want to spend as much time as possible with your players before then. At least there's no more long-distance travelling to be done.

After forty minutes you've cleared your in-tray and start shuffling papers back into your top drawer for safe-keeping – when you notice the small cassette recorder that was used to pick up Steve's conversation. When you last used it, it was only wound on halfway. Now the tape is almost finished.

More secrets?

You lock your office door, rewind back to the halfway mark, and press play. But the voice captured by the tiny device is the last one on earth you expected to hear.

It's yours.

Turn to 500.

325

Nigel suggests you take the middle flight. Turn to 298.

326

There are a couple more questions which you have no trouble batting away; one about the quality of refereeing – 'Only video evidence will tell, but I thought he did a professional job tonight' –

and another about the temperament of one of your players – 'He's passionate about his football and sometimes gets a little excited, that's all.' Bread and butter to a manager like you.

Then an awkward question about the Hardwick Three (as they are still calling them), and you decide it's time to stop the questions. One slip of the tongue on that subject and every lawyer and his dog will be wanting a sniff, and you're certainly not about to tell them it was very nearly the Hardwick Four. No: best keep it all 'between the players and the club following a full inquiry' for now.

Turn to 150.

327

The lab samples are taken, and less than two hours before the match you are informed that Steven Fitzgerald's blood has been found to contain nandrolone steroid. Both samples have been independently checked and no mistakes have been made. With that sort of hole in Hardwick's defence, and the way the news affects the rest of the team, you stand no chance in Europe. Criminals 1, Hardwick 0 – but there will be no match report this time. Turn to 101.

328

You leave the restaurant and make your way back to the club. You have work to do before you can return home.

On a normal Friday you would still expect to see quite a few people milling around the club, working late into the night to ensure everything runs smoothly for the Saturday match. But tonight the grounds are deserted and the building silent. You make your way to your office, feeling a little tense, and lock the door behind you. It's not worth taking chances.

You slide open your desk drawer and take out the small box of fingerprinting equipment supplied to you by Higson. You line up the contents in front of you: the jar of black powder, the small, soft-bristled brush, and the white gloves. Next to these you place the item you took from the restaurant.

You pull on the gloves to make sure you don't smudge the prints. You unstop the jar, tilt it over the object and tap firmly. A small amount of powder falls out in a neat pile. You take up the brush and begin dusting the powder around, covering all the areas you think Steve's fingers might have touched. When you have finished, you hold up the object in front of you and blow. A cloud of fine powder floats to the floor, and left behind on the object is a thin covering of dust.

But which object are you working on?

The glass?　　　　　　(Turn to 43)

The cutlery?　　　　　(Turn to 369)

The napkin?　　　　　(Turn to 443)

329

You have a short post-match briefing with your players before sending them home for the night. And you are about to lock up when you spot an envelope on the floor. Someone must have dropped it by accident, but you didn't see who. It has been neatly ripped open along the top, but is otherwise blank. Do

you take it (turn to 346)? Or leave it and go home (turn to 149)?

330
Are Zaki Roberts and Ant Bostock on the field at this moment? If so, turn to 454. If not, turn to 402.

331
Who are your opponents in this match?
Real Sabadell?	(Turn to 73)
Noordenhaarcnijk?	(Turn to 232)
Cochons d'Inde?	(Turn to 165)

332
Are you trying to get this book over with or something? If you're *really* too busy to talk to the players concerned, turn to 39. If you've changed your mind and would like to talk to them after all, this author's in a good mood: turn to 310.

333
You formulate your training plan for the week, concentrating on crossing, headers and goal shots. You may add **1** to your Attack score for the next match only. Turn to 102.

334
You'd noticed in training that these two have been linking up really well lately, and tonight it looks like it might have paid off.

Ant Bostock receives a wide cross on the right of midfield, and begins a loping diagonal run towards goal. You have three more men up front keeping the defenders occupied, and this allows Jed Stevens to suddenly change direction and dart into the box. Luis

Covas is closing Bostock down, but at exactly the right moment he slots a keen through-ball to Jed, who steadies it with one touch and makes to shoot with his next.

Some would say the goalie does the right thing. It's one on one, and he races out to meet the looming figure of your striker. As Jed's boot connects, the keeper dives at his feet to claim the ball. There is a clash of bodies and Jed is skittled. All together, the home crowd get to their feet and politely share their observations with the referee.

But what will he do? Roll one dice.

If you roll 1–5, turn to 201.

If you roll 6, turn to 549.

335

Your chosen keeper is attentive to the extra training and his ability increases noticeably. You may add **1** to this keeper's Skill for the next **two** matches only. Make a careful note of this on your Fact Sheet. Your training routine this week just might alter the course of history.

When you're ready, turn to 278.

336

The opposition goalkeeper is extremely talented, and plays with a Skill of **5**. This will be important when you're rolling to see if your shot has been saved (see page 24 for a reminder).

Now play out this match as usual. When you reach the 45th minute, turn to 330.

337

You think back to your conversation last week with Higson and remember what he said about your vitamin theory, which frankly seems less and less plausible the more you think about it.

'Have you even talked to the doctor yet?' he had asked you. Perhaps this is your chance. Do you want to have a quiet chat about the drug test results with Heather McCullough, the team doctor (turn to 259), or not (turn to 320)?

338

Saturday 8th, 10:30 a.m.
As before, the draw will be shown live by satellite at the club. Your presence is expected by everyone – there is an electric feeling running through the whole club that this year might just be the one, and that you might just be the manager to do it. Anyway you wouldn't miss it for the world.

But that doesn't mean you're not nervous. There's no chaff at this stage, and any team who has got this far hasn't done it just by riding their luck; they are all shining examples of dedicated, exceptional football teams, and although you can proudly count yourself in this list you know you'll be up against it when the first leg kicks off on Tuesday.

You are one of the last to enter the boardroom this time, which is packed as always but a seat has been reserved for you at the front. When people notice you enter, a round of applause ripples across the room, and several people clap you on the back as you make your way to your seat. You smile at them, and someone at the back shouts out 'Here we go again!' as the screen flickers and the familiar faces of the UEFA officials appear once more.

Turn to 497.

339

'Hurry past, lads. They're vultures this lot. Don't worry, your bags will catch you up.'

You lead the way and there is a flurry of notebooks and cameras as the waiting journalists jockey for position in their roped-off area.

'What's your position on drug-taking in sport?'

'Can you really compete without the Hardwick Three?'

'How are you punishing your players?'

The questions come thick and fast, but you stubbornly ignore them and quicken your pace. Before long you and your players are safe behind the closed doors of the bus, on your way to the waiting aeroplane. Turn to 517.

340

You busy yourself in the familiar safety of your office. After fifteen minutes you are startled by a sharp knocking on your door, even though you knew it was coming.

'Good morning, Nigel.' You greet your chairman and usher him inside. You are hardly surprised to see Heather McCullough behind him, and you politely hold the door open as she follows him in. He has a grave expression, while she looks faintly triumphant.

'I won't mess about,' Nigel says bleakly. 'Dr McCullough has very grave allegations against you – I believe you know what they are – and unless you have a very good explanation, I will have to move towards your immediate suspension.'

'Really? I'd like to hear them from Dr McCullough first,' you tell him.

'That won't be necessary,' she says, slowly chewing her gum behind a cold smile. 'You can hear it in your very own words.'

She pulls out a small cassette recorder, presses play and places it on the desk between you. Counter-espionage! This dictaphone was in her pocket all along, and it recorded everything you said to her. You sit and listen to your conversation earlier in Heather's office.

'This is very serious,' Nigel Douglas tells you, lifting up his glasses and pinching the bridge of his nose tiredly. 'Do you have anything you want to add?'

Have you just brought something up from the incinerator? If so, turn to 157. If not, turn to 287.

341

Your whole body stiffens, and you suddenly feel like a rabbit caught in headlights. How did this happen? You haven't even done anything wrong, yet here you are feeling like the guilty party. Your heart thumps high in your chest and Heather McCullough's voice sounds distant as she leaves a voicemail for the club chairman.

Pull yourself together – that means he hasn't arrived yet, so you have time to think. Did you bug Heather's office last night? If so, turn to 255. If not, turn to 181.

342

The Bayern goalie, Ray Richards, is in top form and plays with a Skill of 6. This will be important when you are rolling to see if he has saved your shot (see page 24 for a reminder).

But what about your keeper? Have you picked Jamie Coates for this match? If so, turn to 224. If not, turn to 307.

343

By now you should know the full name of the person who is behind this campaign of terror. Without this information you don't stand a chance. Turn to 101.

344

The players know they're going to have to improve fast.

'If that's the best I thought you could do,' you continue in a softer tone, 'I wouldn't have brought you here. I'd have saved the entry fee and kept you all back for extra gym work. But I'm a fighter. I was born a fighter. I'll fight everyone in this room if I have to.'

Some of your players flinch.

'I know that wasn't the match you lot have been working up to all your careers. And if we're going to pull ourselves out of this barrel of laughs, I'm going to need one hundred and fifty per cent from every one of you. Two hundred in injury time. Now get out there and impress me.'

Good speech! Add **1** Morale, **2** if you're Assertive or Inspirational, and **3** if you're both. See if it's done the trick by turning to 243.

345

A pile of letters, junk mail mostly. There doesn't seem to be anything important. Turn to 320.

346

You scoop up the envelope and pull out a single sheet of creamy paper. It's a little crumpled and has obviously been read several times before. But it's not in English:

GNXR GUR EVTUG SYVTUG. GERNQ BAYL BA ONYYF NAQ JUVFGYRF.

If you've got Bruce Babel on your books at the moment, turn to 302. If not, good luck interpreting it! You might want to make a note of it on your Fact Sheet for later; then you may turn to 149.

347
Did you remove the bug from Heather's office? If so, turn to 457. If it's still there, turn to 324.

348
Are Klaus Wehnert and Ian Leslie both on the field? If so, and your Midfield Skill is 20 or higher, turn to 285. If not, play out the remainder of the match and turn to 384 when it's all over.

349
Where did you learn to be such a good negotiator? You were able to secure your chosen staff member's services for less than you thought. That means you've got money left for another. Go back to 252 and choose someone else to add to your staff list. You can only do this once! If you've already selected two members of staff to join your team, turn to 525.

350
After the loss of some of Hardwick City's key players, the club has never been more in need of new blood. There are three players on the market who catch your attention, and their details are listed over the page.

Bradley Bailey

Skill: 7
Position: Defender
Born: Demoine 9/12/71
Height: 6ft 4in
Weight: 14st 9lb

Last Season's Stats:
Goals: 0
Yellow Cards: 4
Red Cards: 1

You actually met Bradley Bailey for the first time when he drove into the back of you after you'd watched his team play in a tense nil-nil. But you hadn't let that put you off his abilities in defence: he had received the man-of-the-match award that day for a resolute, match-saving performance.

BRADLEY BAILEY

Dimitris Hiotis

Skill: 6
Position: Midfielder
Born: Athens 12/3/85
Height: 5ft 11in
Weight: 12st 10lb

Last Season's Stats:
Goals: 3
Yellow Cards: 5
Red Cards: 0

In the year when Greece were winners of the Euro championship and the Eurovision Song Contest, Dimitris had to choose between football and singing. He chose wisely. He's still young, but like lightning in the midfield and uses the width of the pitch like an old master. Oh, and he does a mean karaoke too.

DIMITRIS HIOTIS

Oriol Aspachs

Skill: 7

Position: Attacker

Born: Barcelona 31/3/78

Height: 5ft 10in

Weight: 11st 10lb

Last Season's Stats:

Goals: 11

Yellow Cards: 3

Red Cards: 0

ORIOL ASPACHS

Oriol is a product of the Barcelona youth academy and he has lived in the city all his life, so his English is a bit shaky. He got the call-up to the Spanish national side last year, but refused because he claims he is not Spanish, but Catalan! This has divided the public in his homeland, but you have to admire his stubbornness. Not to mention his right boot: he holds the record for the only player in history to have kicked the ball so hard it broke the net.

Think carefully. Which areas of your squad most need extra personnel? Before you make any decisions, are you currently employing Eddie Nimrod? If so, you should turn to 357 right now. If not, what do you wish to do?

Make a bid for Bradley Bailey (asking price 5 million)?

(Turn to 403)

Make a bid for Dimitris Hiotis (asking price 7 million)?

(Turn to 358)

Make a bid for Oriol Aspachs (asking price 6 million)?

(Turn to 185)

Consider your other options? (Turn to 250)

351

You decide it's time to give your own players a bit of attention. With only two days remaining before the first big match, this is your opportunity to give them the confidence they need to believe they can win.

You stride purposefully to the dressing room where the players have gathered. But you are not greeted with the cacophony of noise you would normally expect at the beginning of the week, and there is an uneasy hush in the room.

'Keep your voices down, lads!' you joke as you enter.

But their bleak expressions worry you, and no one says anything. You turn to Danny Knox, your dependable team captain.

'Danny, what's going on here?' you ask, more seriously now.

'There's so many of us missing, boss,' Danny Knox tells you awkwardly. 'It just doesn't feel right, since the – drug thing.'

The news of the positive tests has clearly stunned them.

'We're half a team,' says Ant Bostock.

'We haven't got a chance,' Ian Leslie adds with characteristic bluntness.

You're going to have to decide how best to approach this.

If you want to heavily criticise the three guilty players and try to shock the rest of the squad into obedience, turn to 190.

If you'd prefer to stay calm and use your authority to encourage them, turn to 431.

352

You manage to persuade Hans Gross to join the Hardwick payroll. Hans kept goal for the German national side for most of the eighties, and after retirement turned to coaching. He's one of the best! During the competition he will spend time with your goalies, Jamie

Coates and Rob Rose, making them into shot-stopping heroes. You may immediately add **1** to the Skill of one of your goalkeepers (you choose who). Mark this special information under Management Information on your Fact Sheet alongside 'Hans Gross, Goalkeeping Coach', on page 284. When you've done that turn to 480.

353

It doesn't matter how long you're in this game, one thing never changes: away matches are intimidating. Walking out there to thousands of roaring fans is nerve-wracking enough. When they're nearly all cheering for the other team, it's like putting your head in the lion's mouth.

Here are Bayern Badetuch's stats:

Bayern Badetuch
Manager: Kurt Schloss
Formation: 4-5-1
Defence Skill: 22
Midfield Skill: 18
Attack Skill: 17

Transfer this information to your second Match Sheet on page 275. Fill in your own team's information as well.

How's it looking? Think you can grab a shock win here tonight? There's only one way to find out. Turn to 342.

354

Is Bradley Bailey in your line-up? If so, turn to 477. If not, turn to 331.

355

You step out on to the warm tarmac and are whisked off by bus to your hotel in the south of the city. As you arrive and step off the coach, there is a small knot of football supporters wearing all manner of European club shirts, waiting in the hope of catching a glimpse of the quarter-finalists. It's always nice to find the real football fans – the ones who don't care if it's them or us – and you're proud of your players as they chat with the adults and sign footballs for the children.

When everyone has been shown to their rooms and unpacked, the players congregate in the hotel restaurant to eat a specially prepared meal.

'Boss – come and have a look at these cakes. They're amazing!'

You look up to see Danny ushering you in the direction of the chiller cabinets.

'You don't even like cake,' you say. 'Remember that time you threw up on –'

'Boss – the *cakes*. Over *here*.'

You get up from your seat to join Danny on the far side of the restaurant. The other players don't notice you slip away, being too busy trying to explain 'baked beans' to a puzzled waiter.

'What is it, Dan?' The look on your captain's face has you concerned as you both pretend to stare at the gateaux slowly revolving inside a tall glass fridge.

'There's a rumour going round,' he tells you. 'Haven't you noticed the lads are avoiding the subject of the drugs? The missing players?'

· ·

You had noticed and had hoped it was just because they were concentrating on the football. But he's right – they have been quiet recently, and you realise you have been avoiding raising the subject as much as them.

'What rumour?' you ask.

'That there's some sort of conspiracy. That Sal, Will and Antek – they were doped. That it's not their fault. They're saying all sorts. That someone's out to get them, that one of us is next – paranoia, of course, chief, but they need to hear it from you.'

You look at him and see that he needs to hear it from you as well.

Turn to 179.

356

Oriol Aspachs has a little trouble with the language at first, but Babel is very attentive and helps him to make friends at the club. Before long he is speaking like he was born in Hardwick! Great stuff – you've got yourself a bargain in this excellent striker, and it's important that he's happy here. Thank Bruce for his efforts and turn back to 250.

357

You discuss your transfer options with Eddie, who is probably more in tune with the comings and goings of the transfer market than anyone you know.

'I agree with you,' he says. 'All three are very promising players. But I'm wary of Bradley Bailey. He's very fussy, and doesn't travel well. What Hardwick needs now are lads who will settle quickly into the club and get results, not egos in shorts.'

The advice is there, and that's what you pay him for. Whether you take it or leave it is up to you. Armed with Eddie's opinions, you may now go back to 350 and make your decisions.

358

The asking price for Dimitris Hiotis is 7 million. If you want to bid for him, this is what to do. First, decide how much money (in millions) you want to offer. Next, roll one dice and add it to your offer. If the total is higher than his asking price of 7, then you have successfully signed Hiotis on to your team! If it is equal or lower, you have failed. Choose carefully how much to offer, because you only get one go at this. And remember you're not allowed to offer more money than you've got!

If you are Diplomatic, add **1** to the dice roll because you're so good at talking people into things.

If you buy Dimitris Hiotis, add his name to your Squad Details on page 285 and subtract the money you paid from your Budget. Or take some time to think about it if you like. In any case, go back to 250 to consider your options.

359

Add the score from this match to the score from the last match. This will give you your **aggregate total**. Who has the most goals?

You?   (Turn to 372)

Them?   (Turn to 217)

The same?   (Turn to 13)

360

'OK,' you tell him, leaning forward in your chair and refusing to break eye contact. 'Tell me what you have taken then.'

Antek is very quick to speak. 'Vitamins, 500mg. Painkillers for headache, 200mg, twice. Also ginseng for make me wide awake, but that's not steroid. Doctor Heather say all of them ok – you ask her.'

Antek is brisk and precise in his reply.

'Are you sure that's all?' you ask.

'Of course I'm sure.'

Record any information you wish, then turn to 6.

361

'Are you sure this is it?'

'I'm sure,' you say. It's the only one that fits the description, and anyway, whoever owns this place must have made a small fortune at some time or other.

'So what's the plan?'

'Get to the front door without being caught,' you reply, not entirely sure what comes afterwards and trying to sound convincing. 'I'll go first, you follow.'

Turn to 54.

362

They understand. You can tell. Turn to 243.

363

Mbaye is twisting his way through your midfield, leaving it in tatters as he stops and starts his way to goal down the left flank. He has the pick of Noordenhaarenijk's strikers to both sides as he turns on goal, and brings his foot back from twenty yards. There is no knowing if he will cross left, right or have a pop on goal himself.

Roll one dice for Mbaye's shot. Then roll two dice for your Defence (three dice if you have the Flexible quality). If any of your dice match Mbaye's roll, the ball has been kept out; but more by luck than anything else. If neither dice matches, it means the ball has found its way into the net and Noordenhaarenijk have a goal to celebrate. Remember to mark it on your Match Sheet if this happens.

Play out the remainder of the game in the usual way, and when it's all over, turn to 384.

364

'Why would a player take steroids,' Nigel asks, disbelieving, 'knowing that he's absolutely certain to get caught? The players have been tested every week since the first set of positives.'

'Maybe he's being threatened too,' Heather offers.

'No,' you say. 'You can tell by the phone call he's in on this.'

'Then I still don't get it. Why?'

'We should take a vote on it,' Nigel says with conviction. I think we should confront Steve first thing in the morning and demand to know what's going on. He might just panic and spill the beans.'

'No way. I vote we try to find out some other way, without his knowing. We shouldn't tell him anything, just in case.' Heather is just as definite.

Both your colleagues look at you. It's your turn. What course of action is best?

If you agree with Nigel, turn to 214.

If you agree with Heather, turn to 447.

365

'On paper, you just can't separate these two teams.'

'That's true, John. But history tells us that never before has a team beginning with H got further than this stage in the European Cup. Will that statistic still stand in ninety minutes?'

'Who knows, Clive. But more to the point, who cares?'

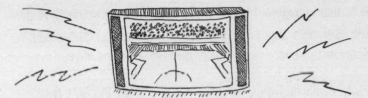

One team will cruelly crash out at this stage, and be remembered by no one; the other will go on to play in the final and have a taste of glory.

Gather your dice and hope it's you. Play out the game as usual; when 90 minutes are up, turn to 154.

366

You know that if Heather's story is true – and she has the photos and blackmail to prove it – she is being used as much as you are. You feel like a pawn in a game. But you also know that the only chance you have is to pool your information, helping each other. And you have one clear advantage: whoever is behind this doesn't know that the three of you are working together. If you can keep pretending Heather is still working for the enemy, you might just have a chance.

'Nigel,' you say gently, turning to your chairman, 'what could

Heather possibly have to gain from this? Remember the threatening letters? I believe her. Sit down. We need to talk this through.'

Nigel Douglas sits. You can see how much this has upset him, and you feel glad to have a chairman who cares so much about his football club this time.

'Does anyone know who this Greg could be?' he asks.

'Is there anyone else on your team?' you ask.

Heather shakes her head. 'Only I have access to medical. Whoever talked Fitzgerald into this didn't get the dope from me.'

Turn to 364.

367

You slowly climb the stairs which wind and twist through narrow spaces and peculiar angles, forcing you to bend and stoop as you ascend. And then all of a sudden they stop at a blank wall. There is a passage leading right, and another leading left. You pick the one on the left, and follow it round in a clockwise direction. You pass two doors on your right before you are brought full circle back to where you started. The two doors must both lead to a large, circular room. The only other way is down.

If there are two of you, you decide to take a door each. If you're on your own, you head for the nearest door.

Turn to 53.

368

Two of your players have lost some of their ability by doing so much loafing and messing about. Take your pencil, turn to your Squad Details and close your eyes. Both of them. Now pick two players at random, and deduct **1** from each of their Skills.

Get back to work, you muppet. Turn to 411.

369

The polished surface of the knife and fork might be suitable for getting Steve's prints, but they've been handled a lot by him and are very smudgy. Roll one dice. If you roll 1 or 2, turn to 92. If you roll 3–6, turn to 288.

370

Turn to 526.

371

You wait for all your players to traipse off the pitch and into the dressing room. You close the door behind them noiselessly and remain silent for a minute, before exploding.

'I've seen faster zombies,' you begin. Eleven pairs of eyes are lowered, embarrassed.

'I've seen a dead dog who could play you lot off the park today. I've seen stronger schoolgirls.'

John Hoggart looks up.

'My sister's still at school and actually she's very –'

'LEAVE IT, HOGWASH!' you roar, glaring at him. 'Anyone else want to make a stupid comment or do you accept that *that* was totally, completely awful?'

You indicate in the direction of the pitch. No one says a word.

Are you at least two goals down in the match? If you are, turn to 344. If it's not that bad, turn to 2.

372

You did it! Your coaching staff leap from their seats as the ref's whistle is blown, and several players rush to greet them on the touchline. There are hugs and back slaps all round, and the noise of the fans fills your ears from the packed visitors' stand to your right. For the first time in the club's history, Hardwick have reached the semis of the most prestigious tournament in club football. You stride over to pump the hand of your captain, who is looking ecstatic at the result.

'We did it, guv,' he is saying. 'We're still a strong team. There's no stopping us now!'

You have no trouble beaming now, lost in the excitement of the moment. But it's only the semis, and there is still work to do. Lead your exalted squad in a show of appreciation to the fans – where would these overpaid young men be without fans? – and make your way back to home turf by turning to 275.

373

Hmm. You seem to have gone a bit soft. That sort of spiel would be suitable to a more balanced game, but this match is rather beyond that. Lose **1** Morale. Lose another **1** if you have the Assertive quality, as this was far from it.

Now turn to 243.

374

You scroll down the text, and using the codebreaker you found on the postcard in Steve's locker, decipher the following message:

Access now by fingerprint: only us 3. Anything else alerts security. Make sure CX-90 device secure in locker room B4 U come over. C U in 2 days 4 meeting.

The text was sent last week, so that meeting has already happened. But what are they talking about? Access to where by fingerprint?

Who are the three? And what's this device they're talking about? Better make a note of everything you've read on your Fact Sheet before returning to 86.

375

You drive to Woodborough to investigate the address. You look all over the town and stop three times to ask for directions, but no one has heard of West End Mansion. You must have missed something, and this information is crucial to unmasking the individual who is determined to bring down your club. Turn to 101.

376

Sometimes a team just switches off for a few crucial moments. Usually it doesn't really matter, and no one notices. But when the opposition are this strong, they can exploit any weakness. And that's what happens to you now.

There is a brief tussle for a ball on the near side, right in front of you. Your player wins the ball, but under pressure he plays it back to your defenders. His ball is much too short, and your left back has stopped concentrating just for a second; but that's all it takes as the ball is collected by their winger on the gallop. Your defence is back-pedalling in clumsy disarray, and you are almost relieved when someone sticks out a boot in a last-minute tackle and the opposition player goes sprawling.

Your relief gives way to panic as you see the referee run over to the challenger and reach into his top pocket. Roll two dice. Add **1** to your roll if you are Instinctive, as this has encouraged your players to play a natural game; and add another **1** if you are Flexible, because your players will have been better able to resist this sudden siege.

What did you roll?

2 or 3?	(Turn to 463)
4 or 5?	(Turn to 475)
6?	(Turn to 167)
7 or more?	(Turn to 260)

377

Putting the final pieces in this jigsaw will be impossible unless you investigate that address. By choosing not to, you have just sealed Hardwick's fate. If by any chance you can remember the number of the last paragraph, or you've still got your finger keeping your place – you little cheat! – you may turn back and choose again. If not, you're going to have to admit defeat this time. Turn to 101.

378

Did you get more goals in the last match than they got in this match?

If so, turn to 204.

If not, turn to 435.

If you both scored the same number of away goals, turn to 487.

379

You thank the staff for a lovely meal and leave the restaurant. Tomorrow your work begins again in earnest. Turn to 408.

380

You are quick to turn to your team captain Danny Knox and shake his hand. He is grinning, clearly relishing the prospect of a really tough match next week.

As you rise from your chair you feel a hand on your shoulder.

'At least we're at home to start with!' says Nigel Douglas in an upbeat voice. The club's troubles are forgotten for the time being, and your chairman looks relaxed and proud. He leans in to give your hand a good encouraging shake. Your left hand, of course; but you're getting used to this little quirk by now.

Here's how it works. The quarter-final match is played over two legs: the first will be at home at Hardwick's ground, and the second will be away in Europe three days later. The scores of the two matches are then added together to give an aggregate total, and whoever has scored the most goals is the winner. If you and your opponents score the same number in total, the away goal rule is used. It's harder to score goals when you're playing away, so they count double. You'll need to make sure your defence is especially solid at home as a clean sheet is worth its weight in gold!

Several of the staff and players clap you on the back as you leave the meeting room. Your players follow you out and into the dressing room for the morning meeting.

Turn to 26.

381

You turn on the computer, log into the club system and type 'Hexabulin' into the search window. It finds several thousand references, and you're left in no doubt as to what this stuff is.

'This anabolic steroid is detectable in screening tests for up to a year,' one website reads. 'This makes Hexabulin and other nandrolone products off-limits to many competitive athletes.'

Nandrolone anabolic steroid. One of the most powerful muscle-gain pills in existence and completely illegal for any footballer playing under UEFA regulations. But everyone knows this – so why have they been ordered specially? You feel a chill as you realise this could not possibly be a mistake.

You're in up to your neck now. Look through the rest of the drawers by turning to 91.

382

Play out the rest of the match as normal. When 90 minutes are up, turn to 359.

383

You walk to your office and for once things have gone exactly as planned. Lying in the tray of the fax machine is a single sheet of paper, confirming that all players tested earlier today have given clean results. The sheet is signed and countersigned by Dylan and Elliot Bastos, and with a smile you wonder if they do each other's signature as well.

Fold it up and put it in your pocket. Now turn to 439.

384

So, are you living the dream? Or did you have a nightmare? Better get your best managerial smile on – there's a press conference about to start in the club's boardroom. Turn to 524.

385

Abdou Mbaye has found his rhythm in this game and is imposing his talents on the midfield. Your man on the left of midfield commits himself to an aggressive tackle, but Mbaye simply sidesteps and moves up a gear, charging forward into space.

Are Dmitri Duval and Carlos de Carvalho both on the field at this moment? If so, turn to 289. If not, turn to 363.

386

Heather thinks for a moment, then suggests you take the right flight. Turn to 263.

387

You push open the door to the meeting room, which is bare except for a round table and six chairs. Heather McCullough and Nigel Douglas are both sitting facing the door and there is a tense silence.

'I have news,' you tell them both, and begin explaining everything. It's actually a big relief to be able to talk about it. But as soon as you get to the bit about Steve taking the dope himself, Nigel leaps to his feet.

'I knew it – she's double-crossed us,' he splutters.

'I know nothing about it!' Heather demands, half rising from her own seat.

'I think you should both keep your voices down,' you tell them sternly, closing the door behind you. 'There's enough scandal in this club to last a lifetime without telling the world the management have fallen out.'

'Oh, so this is just a coincidence, is it?' Nigel asks sarcastically. 'You expect me to believe –'

'Please,' you implore. 'We had an agreement. Dr McCullough has been threatened. Let her speak.'

'I had no instructions to supply Fitzgerald with steroids. Since that second note I've heard nothing, I thought that was the end of it. This is as much a shock to me as to you.'

There is a long silence and your mind whirrs, going through the possibilities. What do you do?

If you decide enough is enough, call the police and put an end to the Heather's game-playing by turning to 484.

If you'd rather give her the benefit of the doubt – again – turn to 366.

388

TEAM PROFILE
Revolyutsiya Apelsyn
Ukraine

Revolyutsiya are only the second Ukrainian side to qualify for the European League Cup in its history. Their achievement is being trumpeted by the local press as if they'd already won the cup. But although they are good on home territory, they are not expected to advance very far. They are a very energetic side with some excellent individual talent, but defensively they are loose and a well-disciplined opposition with a balanced formation should be able to unravel them at the back.

Star Player: Igor Yuschenko
Winger

When asked to name two famous Ukrainians, most people only get this far. Igor has almost godlike status in his home country and some people have even tipped him to be president one day. He's like lightning down the left wing, and you never know if he's going

IGOR YUSCHENKO

to scoop a danger ball into the box or dart inside his marker and have a pop himself. He's unpredictable, aggressive and so charming off the field that one female reporter actually fainted during an interview with him. He caught her.

When you've digested this information, turn to 351.

389

What's your response? Do you say:

'I'm absolutely 100 per cent opposed to all forms of substance abuse in football. You take drugs, it's early doors.'? (Turn to 452)

Or would you prefer to say:

'It is every sportsman's choice. If he decides to abuse himself and gets caught, well, that's his problem.'?   (Turn to 207)

390

You plan to spend a good deal of your time with your chosen midfielder, focussing on maximising the width of the pitch and controlling the flow and pace of the game. Roll two dice. If you roll doubles, turn to 49. If not, turn to 168.

391

Feels like a draw, doesn't it? It's not. Their goals were away goals, and that's enough to send you crashing out of the cup this time; the cruel truth is written all over the face of the opposition manager as he steps over to shake your hand.

On top you're smiling bravely. Underneath you're sick as a dog. Turn to 101.

392

Homens da Guerra 2(1) v Real Sabadell 0(1)

Noordenhaarenijk 1(2) v **Liblonec Vyoslav** 3(0)

Lazzaro di Savena 1(1) v Kött Fotbollar 0(1)

First leg scores are in brackets, so add them together to get the aggregate totals. When you have finished, turn to 206.

393

TEAM PROFILE
Cochons d'Inde
France

They're not big on scoring, averaging just over a goal a game last season; but Cochons' defence is even more legendary than a certain North London club's used to be. They just have that annoying habit of always being there. Beat one, and another one pops up to take the ball; carefully craft an attacking plan in the secrecy of the classroom, only to find they seem to know exactly what you're up to. Only the best passing and attacking moves undo a back line like this.

Star Player: Meursault
Central Defender

MEURSAULT

He must have a first name, it's just that no one knows what it is. Most people think he was embarrassed about it, but when he became famous and everyone started speculating, he enjoyed the attention too much to let it slip. The thing about Meursault is he seems to play a completely emotionless game. He is absolutely decisive in the box, and can take the ball from an attacker's feet as if he didn't exist. But he's no stranger to controversy either, and even when the ref judges him guilty he can never see that he's done anything wrong.

Turn to 155.

394

Decide carefully how you want to pick your players for this match. If you are happy to sit back and defend an advantage, you might want to rest your best attacking players this time. If you think away goals could be the key to your progress in this cup, pile on the pressure up front – but don't leave gaping holes at the back.

Select your team now. When you have done that, turn to 354.

395

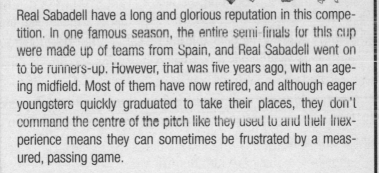

TEAM PROFILE
Real Sabadell
Spain

Real Sabadell have a long and glorious reputation in this competition. In one famous season, the entire semi-finals for this cup were made up of teams from Spain, and Real Sabadell went on to be runners-up. However, that was five years ago, with an ageing midfield. Most of them have now retired, and although eager youngsters quickly graduated to take their places, they don't command the centre of the pitch like they used to and their inexperience means they can sometimes be frustrated by a measured, passing game.

Star Player: Claudio Casimiro
Striker

His name means 'lame, peaceful one'. In your dreams. Speed is the key with Casimiro, and nothing shows it better than his performance last season when he was responsible for winning twice as many penalties as any other team in La Liga. Defenders just can't cope with him as he turns one way then the other, and he's always on the lookout for a stray boot to bring him down. He's equally deadly on goal as well, and your defence will have to be on fine form if Claudio is to be kept at bay.

CLAUDIO CASIMIRO

Turn to 155.

396

'Well, lads,' you say in a loud voice over the noise of the dressing room. 'Here we are again. You've shown me what you can do in training this week. Do it on the field tonight and I'll not ask for more. These Swedes are a class act, but this is a match like any other and I want you all singing from the same song sheet tonight.'

Ant Bostock digs Carlos de Carvalho in the ribs and he lets out a high-pitched squeal. You roll your eyes.

'Play for your shirt, and remember the three Ts: Tight, Tidy and . . .' Oh God – you've forgotten what the third T is. Better make it up quickly. Is it:

Tempo?	(Turn to 540)
Tactical?	(Turn to 494)
Tedious?	(Turn to 481)

397

You have chosen the quality of Assertiveness. This means you are a decision-maker and self-assured, and occasionally you might even be able to psyche out the opposition. But it means you can be a bit of a bully. Assertiveness could work for or against you depending on what situations you find yourself in! You'll get special instructions about all this later in the book. For the time being, simply write 'Assertiveness' on your Fact Sheet on page 284 under Manager Qualities. Then turn to 209.

398

Your chosen keeper has reacted tremendously well to the extra attention, and you may add **1** to his Skill on a permanent basis. Make a note of this on your Fact Sheet.

Good work! That's what they pay you for, and Hardwick are in a much stronger position now thanks to your shrewd management. Consider doing a few credit card adverts, then turn to 278.

399

What was the result?

If you won, turn to 239.

If it was a scoreless draw (nil-nil), turn to 267.

If it was a scoring draw, turn to 160.

If you lost, turn to 67.

400

There's more: the ref is pulling out his book and taking out a card – it's red! The keeper's off! The captain is arguing, but what's the point? The little man in black is God, and he layeth down the law.

Remember to reduce their Skill by 5 for the rest of the match due to this sending off (refer to page 25 if you want). Now take the penalty as you usually would, but add **1** to your dice roll because they can't use their first-choice keeper any more.

Did that go well? Mark it up on the Match Sheet if it did. Then turn to 304.

401

Danny's shot makes the goalkeeper look like a statue. Your striker waits until he sees the ball beat the keeper's outstretched arms, then spins away to run up the field, arm raised in celebration while other Hardwick players mob him from all directions. Beautiful one-touch football, an incredible goal, and priceless away from home. Chalk it up on the card and carry on with the match. When the whistle sounds for full time, turn to 359.

402

The ref sounds the two notes of half time on his whistle, and the opposition manager turns to you with a sneer under his moustache.

'We will destroy you in the second half,' he tells you without a trace of humour. You've never liked him.

'I've heard some dodgy forty-five minute claims,' you reply as you leave the dugout, 'but that's the worst yet.'

As usual, make changes to your team if you wish. As soon as you're ready, play the remainder of the game as normal. When it's all over, turn to 399.

403

Bailey's current team is asking 5 million for his services. Is he worth it? Here's how it works. If you want to buy him, decide how many millions you're willing to pay. Now roll one dice and add it to your offer. If this total is more than his asking price (5 in this case), congratulations: your bid has been accepted! If it is equal or lower, your bid is rejected. You only get one chance at this, so decide carefully – and remember you can't offer more money than you've actually got!

If you possess the Diplomatic managerial quality, you may add **1** to your dice roll as you are very persuasive.

If you buy Bradley Bailey, welcome him to your squad and add his name to your Squad Details on page 285. Don't forget to subtract what you paid from your Budget. If you want more time to think about it, you don't have to make a decision now. Whatever you do, go back to 250 to decide what to do next.

404

'I think we can be sure Hardwick have come here to score goals, John. But who is going to emerge victorious?'

'With two giants of the game like these, Clive, I think the winner tonight will be the game of football.'

The ref tosses a coin in time-honoured fashion, and they get the choice of ends. The ref watches as the two captains shake hands, and the players arrange themselves in their positions, jumping and stretching to keep warm in the cool night air. There is a long pause as the match officials make their final checks, then the whistle is blown and the game is underway! Play the match out as usual and when it's over, turn to 359. If at any point during the match you roll a double six or a double one, turn to 437.

405

After the end of that nasty business with Danny Knox two seasons ago, you had been impressed by DCI Higson of Scotland Yard. He was cautious but meticulous and always fair, and although he had criticised you for getting too involved in a dangerous crime, you had become friends for a while afterwards. But your lives have gone their separate ways since, and you've sometimes found yourself wondering what he's up to these days. He'd know what's for the best at a time like this. Do you want to try to get in touch with him? If so, turn to 176. If you'd rather leave him alone and not get involved in any of this, turn to 422.

406

'I've never seen anything like it,' you say in a low whisper.

'Me neither,' comes the reply. 'Are you sure you know what you're doing?'

Good question. Do you? You need to get to those stairs. Who is going to decide how? If it's you, turn to 418. If it's your companion, turn to 486.

407

The individual concerned plays for Cochons d'Inde, and he is out because of a 'bony growth' on his ankle. What is it with athletes and bony growths? More importantly, are Cochons d'Inde your opponents tomorrow night? If so, turn to 409. Otherwise you touch down smoothly at your destination; turn to 355.

408

You try to spend as much time with your team as possible in these few crucial days. It is important that their enthusiasm and skill gradually crescendo during the nail-biting countdown to Saturday's big match, and you hold regular meetings with your players and coaching staff between sessions on the training field.

But you can't help your mind occasionally wandering to other things. Did you send something to Higson in the last few days? If so, turn to 147. If not, turn to 270.

409

Roll one dice. If you roll:
1 or 2, turn to 220
3 or 4, turn to 263
5 or 6, turn to 70

410

Take a look in the mirror. Do you like what you see? You should have a much better idea now of where your strengths (and weaknesses!) lie. But be careful. Now you have chosen your character, you must play the part well. If you talk one way but act another, you might find things go against you.

What do you wish to turn your attention to now?

Consider your staffing situation?   (Turn to 184)
Look at your reserve team?   (Turn to 74)
Forget all that and get on with the football?   (Turn to 271)

411

Monday 20th
It's the day before your second match in this tournament. Your

flight over to Flaumiges Badetuch is this afternoon, and the players are filing past you noisily as you sit at the front of the team coach.

'All right, boss', 'Mornin', chief', 'How's it goin', boss?' – at least they're respectful. Well, most of them.

'All right, your highness,' Anthony Bostock calls out, and he ducks as you clip him round the ear. But the atmosphere in the team has improved no end since last week, and for an away match on foreign turf that's exactly what you need. A decent result tomorrow would change the shape of the whole group; it would certainly make next week's game a less nervy affair.

You immerse yourself in thoughts of the tricky match ahead and spend some time studying the information on Bayern Badetuch.

Turn to 40.

412

If you picked a defender, turn to 36.

If a midfielder, turn to 390.

If an attacker, turn to 305.

If you picked one of your goalkeepers, turn to 466.

413

There's a large photograph of you at the airport on the back page of one of the British tabloids – it's rather flattering actually – and above it reads the headline, 'Hardwick's Hard Road'. The journalist quotes the answers you gave, noting that you 'remained coolly professional in the face of the Hardwick Three scandal' and that you 'are clearly behind your team despite intense pressure'.

Well done – you've kept the wolves at bay for now. But no doubt there will be more questions to come.

The best way to shut them up, of course, is to win all your matches! Best get on with the matter in hand by turning to 426.

414

You ring through to Nigel's office, hoping he hasn't left yet. The phone rings twice and Nigel's voice answers.

'It's me,' you say. 'There's something I need to explain.'

Turn to 295.

415

The players will respond well to your plan and this will give you a special benefit in the next **two** matches only. You now have **3** points which you may divide as you wish between your Defence skill and your Midfield skill. For example, you may wish to add 2 to your Defence and 1 to your Midfield. Note that this does not permanently increase the skill of any of your players.

Make a note of that on your next two Match Sheets and turn to 278.

416

Friday 14th, Match Day 7

Taking a deep breath, you push open the dressing-room door and confidently stride in.

'We have the perceived advantage of playing this leg at our own ground,' you tell the players who have gathered around you. 'Let's make that real. Get the right result tonight and we're in the final. I'm not going to get this far just to kick ourselves in the foot, so what I want to see tonight is –'

Well? What do you want to see?

Crisp, clinical finishing?   (Turn to 9)

A siege mentality?   (Turn to 433)
A match like any other?   (Turn to 172)

417

Is Bruce Babel in your employment? If so, turn to 356. If not, turn to 538.

418

You step up to the floor and inspect the tiles. They are each about a foot square and have been laid individually with small gaps between. There are three tiles in front of you, each bearing a different symbol. Which will you tread on?
The ball?   (Turn to 4)
The rattle?   (Turn to 311)
The boot?   (Turn to 513)

419

Time for a team talk befitting such an important match. How do you play this one?
Cautious?   (Turn to 427)
Confident?   (Turn to 233)

420

The shot is perfect, but so is this keeper. He has closed down the angle, forcing the shot to come in close to his body, but he's also left himself enough distance to react; and as the ball flies past him he throws out a gloved hand and gets just enough on it to push it away for a corner.

Danny looks gutted, but he turns to applaud Jamie's clever long ball. You should applaud them both for some inspiring play. Take the corner in the usual way, but you may add **1** to the roll because of the effect such quality has on all the players.

After that, complete the match in the usual way. When it finishes, turn to 359.

421

'You saved my life in there,' Nigel tells you. 'Let me handle the dog.'

Before you can say anything Nigel runs at the Alsatian, who leaps to meet him in mid-air. Nigel raises his right arm to shield his face, and the dog's powerful jaws clamp down on it. You hear a dreadful cracking as his arm breaks under the pressure, and there is a yelp of agony.

You know that your only chance now is to take out the man, and you shout loudly as you shoulder charge him in the midriff. He winces as you both fall to the ground, and as you roll over and over you hope that dog was his only weapon tonight.

The man ends up on top of you underneath a towering apple tree, and as he raises his fist you see the heavy fruit glistening in the moonlight. You bring your knee up into his groin and his face freezes in agony. You roll over one more time, grab his collar and push him away from you as hard as you can. There is another crack as the man's head hits the thick trunk of the tree and his eyes roll into the back of his head. He doesn't move.

You get up and spin round, expecting to see the dog pouncing on you from Nigel's broken body. What you actually see is your chairman getting himself up and dusting off his shirt. The dog is cowering by the side of the house, blood pouring from its shattered teeth. That cracking sound wasn't Nigel's arm breaking after all; it was the dog's teeth splintering.

'Lost it when I was a kid. This is prosthetic,' Nigel says, rapping his knuckles on his right forearm. 'State of the art. Lightweight, but hard as nails.'

'So that's why you always shake hands with your left,' you say.

Nigel shrugs. 'Freaks some people out the first time they shake it.'

'I never knew,' you tell him honestly.

'You never asked.'

You help him up and the two of you run down the drive, exhausted but elated, to your abandoned car.

It's a glorious day.

Turn to 158.

422

You've been so busy this morning that you forgot to have any breakfast, and your protesting stomach tells you it's already nearly lunchtime. Your players – the ones who aren't pumped to the gills on steroids – will be arriving for training soon, and you'll need to focus your mind on next Tuesday's football match.

Before that, you have a short time to consider the state of the transfer market. If you wish to look into your options on buying new players – and perhaps selling a few of your own – turn to 250. If you want to just wait for the players to arrive and begin their training schedule, turn to 521.

423

Score 1 point for your answer. Jot this down somewhere on your Fact Sheet (page 284) – you'll need to refer to it later. Now turn to 128.

424

The players will respond well to your plan and this will give you a special benefit in the next **two** matches only. You now have **3** points which you may divide as you wish between your Attack skill and your Midfield skill. For example, you may wish to add **2** to your Attack and **1** to your Midfield. Note that this does not permanently increase the skill of any of your players.

Make a note of that on your next two Match Sheets and turn to 278.

425

Better make this quick. What are you going to look for?

Text messages? (Turn to 86)
Recent calls? (Turn to 77)

426

Pick your team now. Do it carefully: what is the best way through this German side? Are you planning an all-out offensive? Or is it better to shore up your defences and try to keep them from scoring?

The choice, as always, is yours to make. When you're ready, turn to 353.

427

'We've come this far,' you tell your assembled squad, holding your arms wide to demonstrate just how far you've come. 'We've as good a chance as any at this stage. But all we've built is a house of cards. Lose your will to win and it could come tumbling down at any moment. I'm not prepared to gamble all our eggs on one match. That's why I want you lot' – here you point to your defenders – 'watching every ball, every movement; and you lot' – you indicate your midfield – 'working like there's a chimney on you. I want these defenders out of a job.'

'What about us?' Jed speaks for all your attackers.

You fix him with a wilful glare and take a slow kick at an imaginary ball.

'Back of the net,' you say.

For once Jed understands you perfectly, and all your strikers nod vigorously. But your caution has encouraged your players to play it safe this evening; add **1** to your Defence Skill for this match only, and a further 1 if you have the Tactical quality.

When you're ready to kick off, turn to 336.

428
Turn to 465.

429
You and Nigel enter your office and close the door behind you. A few minutes later there is a soft knock at the door and Heather joins you.

'We've got this far,' she says, sitting down, 'but these people are dangerous. We'll have to tread very carefully now.'

'We should pool our information,' Nigel suggests, nodding in agreement. 'Is anyone any further in figuring out what's going on?'

Two pairs of eyes turn to you.

Do you want to reveal everything you know (turn to 450)? Or would you rather keep things to yourself for now (turn to 474)?

430

Here is the result of tonight's other semi-final (first leg scores in brackets).

```
Homens da Guerra 0(1) v Liblonec Vyoslav 1(0)
    Homens da Guerra win 4 — 3 on penalties
```

Turn to 22.

431

You realise there's no point in getting angry, and take a deep breath as you address your squad.

'What's done is done, and can't be undone,' you begin. 'But I've been in this game longer than most of you have had hot dinners. And I'll tell you one thing: the cast may change, but the script stays the same. The club will investigate the test results, and I will personally speak to each player. But this is a football club, you are football players, and tomorrow night there's a game of football to be won. Your only goal now is to keep performing over and over and over again. Now let's get this ship back on the rails and focus on the job in hand.'

Fifteen pairs of eyes are fixed on you, and you look around the room at Jamie Coates, Carlos de Carvalho, Ben Parker. Expressions have certainly mellowed since you entered the room, and you smell a whiff of optimism.

It's going to take more than one speech to get this team back to the frame of mind they were in yesterday, but for now – nice going! You've done what you're here to do. Add **1** to your Morale. If you have the Inspirational Quality, you can make that **2** as they really took your words to heart. Turn to 236.

432

This isn't easy is it? Look at the match between these two teams. If that match was a draw, turn to 244. Otherwise, put whoever won it first and turn to 139.

433

The players have been around long enough to know what you mean: don't take any chances and concentrate on keeping the ball out of your own net.

Which might be fine if you're already ahead. Did you win the away leg of this match? If so, add **1** to your Defence Skill for this match as your defenders will give you at least a hundred per cent. But if not, this is a bad move. You need to score goals, and this isn't the way to do it: subtract **3** from your Attack Skill instead.

Ready? Let's hope so. Turn to 365 to kick off.

434

The pressure pad under the tile is immediately activated, and you don't make it any further. There is a loud *thunk* as the front door locks itself, followed immediately by a loud whooping alarm that resounds deafeningly around the hard walls and floor. Down the stairs come men. With dogs. And baseball bats.

It's not pretty. Turn to 101.

435

Here lies the manager of Hardwick City. All that work, and the cup could hardly have been closer; but in the end, Steve and Greg will be the ones celebrating tonight.

Turn to 101.

436

One of your players has suffered a setback. With such little practice on the pitch, ability will quickly deteriorate. Take a pencil, turn to your Squad Details and close your eyes. Pick one of your players at random and deduct **1** from his Skill.

Ashamed of yourself? You should be. Turn to 411.

437

Did you roll double six (turn to 215) or double one (turn to 376)?

438

Are you in possession of a bugging device? If so, and you wish to use it now, turn to 483. Otherwise leave the office as you found it and drive home for the night. You can confront Heather in the morning: turn to 523.

439

In the Hardwick dressing room, the players are in a noisily happy mood. For tonight, the drug scandal is all but forgotten; you have guided the team through to a serious stage in this competition, and for that you are roundly applauded by every player as you step through the door. You grin at them and raise your hands above your head to clap them right back.

'There are plenty of good players out there who have an abundance of talent and all the shots in the world,' you tell the smiling crowd, 'but at the end of the day it is the committed, focused, honest, courageous and selfless players who make the grade. When I first came to Hardwick –'

'Boss,' Danny Knox interrupts, getting up and putting an arm round your shoulders, 'we're already through to the quarters.

How about you save the speech and buy us all a drink?'

Everyone laughs, including you as you realise how long it's been since you actually relaxed.

Do you go for a drink with the lads? If so, turn to 508. If not, you'd better have a good excuse – if you have a meeting you wish to attend, go there by turning to the room number it's being held in. If you'd just prefer not to go, turn to 249.

440

You press your finger against the screen and hear a series of soft clicks from behind the panel – your heart thuds frantically in your chest as you wait. Then two words are displayed in soft green letters: WELCOME, STEVE. You try the handle, and the door swings open.

Turn to 451.

441

Have you figured it out yet? Consider what you've just found out. Your own voice somehow finds its way from your office, through someone else's bug (stuck on with chewing gum), into your own bug and back to your office again . . .

When the penny drops, take the first name of the person who must have planted the bug. Then convert the letters of their name into numbers: a=1, b=2, c=3, etc. Add these numbers up and turn to that paragraph. If you just can't work it out, turn your attention to the semi-final match by going to 457.

442

Nigel makes it to the foot of the staircase in perfect safety.

'No problem,' he hisses. 'I don't think it was even a trap.'

You quickly follow the path he took to join him. Turn to 174.

443

The napkin is useless for this sort of thing. You need a smooth surface to get proper fingerprints, and the powder has just made smudgy stains on the cloth. Better clean up your office and return home for the night. Turn to 408.

444

'Oh my God!' She nearly spits out her chewing gum in surprise. 'You scared me – what the hell are you doing here in the dark?'

'Sit down, Heather. I think you know exactly why I'm here,' you tell her sternly.

She sits, takes a deep breath, and looks at you. You are completely shocked by what she says next.

'No, I'm sorry. I have no idea. I suggest you explain yourself immediately, unless you want the board to find out about this.'

You were expecting an immediate confession, or some sort of guilty response. Better get straight to the point.

'It's over, Heather. I was in here last night and I've seen the evidence. I know what you've been doing.'

Dr McCullough raises her eyebrows.

'I have absolutely no idea what you're talking about. Get out immediately.'

'Open your desk drawer now,' you roar, 'because I cannot wait to hear your explanation.'

Heather flinches, but keeps her gaze fixed on you. There is a brief pause, and Heather smiles politely. 'Very well.'

She opens the drawer and begins to take out items one by one, placing them on her desk just as you did a few hours ago.

Only this time they are not the same objects.

'Stapler,' she says, as she puts a small stapler in front of you. 'Ballpoint pen, calculator, stethoscope, blood pressure monitor. Oh, and a paperweight, made by my six-year-old daughter. I suppose you want to interrogate her too?'

She spits out this last sentence, but manages to stay calm. You, on the other hand, can feel the blood draining from your face as you look at the row of innocuous objects on the desk between you. You lunge across the desk and pull both drawers open to their full extent. They are empty. The pills, the catalogue, the mortar and pestle – all gone. You look up at Heather, your eyes widening, as you realise the tables have been turned. You begin to wonder if you imagined it all – the stresses of work, lack of sleep – are you ill? Did you make it up? But these thoughts will have to wait, because Dr McCullough has picked up the phone and dialled a number.

'Let's see what Nigel Douglas has to say about this,' she snarls.
Turn to 341.

445

You drive to Calverton to investigate the address. You look all over the town and stop three times to ask for directions, but no one has heard of East End Mansion. You must have missed something, and this information is crucial to unmasking the individual who is determined to bring down your club. Turn to 101.

446

All three players were behaving pretty oddly. Will Frost's shifty awkwardness; Salvatore Duce's aggressiveness; and Antek Bobak's offended anger. Of course, no two players are the same. But not one of them admitted to taking anything illegal. And not only that:

none of them offered an explanation of just *how* a substance like nandrolone ended up in their bloodstreams in the first place. You don't just take it accidentally, or catch it like a cold.

Of course, they might all be lying. It wouldn't be the first time you've been lied to, and if you think this is the case now turn to 68. Or are you more suspicious? If you think you've got something else to go on, turn to 100.

447

'Heather's right,' you say, turning to Nigel. 'We only have a chance if we can find out what he's up to without his knowing.'

'And how do you suggest we do that?' your chairman asks.

'We keep our eyes and ears open,' you say. 'Anything suspicious, when he leaves, when he arrives.'

'We have to find out more,' Heather says. 'With only a first name to go on, we've got nothing.'

'Anyone checked his locker?' Nigel asks.

Turn to 234.

448

Turn to 434.

449

Score 1 point for this answer. Make a note of this somewhere on your Fact Sheet (page 284) as you'll be told to add them up later. Now turn to 128.

450

You tell Nigel and Heather everything you know, piece by piece. When you have finished, you sit back in your chair, feeling better that two other people now know what you know.

Three, actually. Because underneath your desk, embedded in a wad of freshly-chewed gum, is a tiny microphone – the kind you might have seen before – and it has just relayed your entire speech to the criminal mastermind himself. Knowledge is power, and by throwing it around so easily you have tipped the balance in favour of your enemy. They will make sure your investigations come to an abrupt end: you have failed.

Turn to 101.

451

You find yourself in a cavernous hall. Either side of you is a row of six thick granite pillars, supporting a ceiling at least fifteen feet above your head. Beyond these are walls covered with oil portraits, the kind whose eyes you expect to move. They don't; not while you're looking at them anyway. The floor in front of you is covered by a raised dais made from polished marble tiles, decorated with symbols and stretching from one wall to the other. There are four types of tile: balls, boots, rattles and whistles. Beyond this are stairs. There are no other exits, and the room is utterly silent.

What a very peculiar place. Are you alone (turn to 418), or are there two of you here (turn to 406)?

452

Score 2 points for this answer. You'll need to tot these up later, so make a note somewhere on your Fact Sheet (page 284). Now turn to 128.

453

Heather walks up to the tiled area and steps out gingerly. She puts her whole weight on one of the tiles, then another, then another. You stay behind her, matching her every step. By and by you both reach the other side. Turn to 174.

454

True, it was a stop-start first half, but somehow the fourth official has decided there will be a full four minutes of added time. No manager likes injury time; it's when bad things happen. So much has happened in the last four weeks, and you wonder what could happen in the next four minutes.

And then it does happen. In a brilliant display of bravery, Zaki takes the ball cleanly from his opposite number on the left of midfield. All the momentum had been with the other team until then, and their players are out of position; not so Roberts and Bostock.

Zaki picks up the pace, and skips neatly over a sliding tackle without dropping a stitch. Suddenly it's two on two, and the defenders are racing back to their line. Zaki waits until he's almost in the area before threading a pass through to Ant Bostock, who has been matching him for pace on the right. Ant controls with one and passes straight back with two; Zaki has sped through the back line and is clear on goal with the ball at his feet again. The keeper has no time to do anything but hope he dives the right way; he doesn't. Roberts thumps his right boot hard into the ball, making sure not to lean back too far. It spins past the opposition no. 1 and curls away into the right-hand corner of the net.

The away stand goes mental, but the defenders have their arms in the air, appealing for the offside. Did Zaki time that run properly or not? Roll two dice. If you roll 6 or more, turn to 265. If you roll 5 or less, turn to 496. If you have the Tactical quality, you may add **1** to your roll as you've practised this attacking one-two in training.

455

You are a natural leader, and your players look up to you. You inspire confidence and respect in them, and they want to impress you. Your very presence energises your team, and this really pays off when the opposition are flagging or nervous.

If you are ever involved in a match that goes to extra time or – heaven forbid – a dreaded penalty shoot-out, you huddle your team together and make sure that that fighting spirit doesn't fade away.

For all periods of extra time, you may add **2** points each to your Attack, Midfield and Defence scores. And if you ever get to a penalty shoot-out, you'll be given special instructions.

Write all that down on your Fact Sheet on page 284, along with the word 'Inspirational' under Manager Qualities. When you've done that you may turn to 209.

456

Are both Ant Bostock and Jed Stevens on the field? If so, turn to 334. If not, or only one of them is playing at the moment, turn to 304.

457

Two uneventful days pass as you oversee Hardwick's training schedule. You keep a careful eye on all your players, as you must decide which ones get selected for Friday's return leg. Do that now: Match Sheet 7 is on page 281. When you've finished, turn to 536.

458

It's fifteen minutes before kick-off: time to give the team one of your famous pre-match talks. How do you want to play it?

Friendly?	(Turn to 396)
Fiery?	(Turn to 66)

459

You tear open the envelope and read excitedly. It seems you have the choice of a lump sum of £50,000, or £1,000 a year for the rest of your life. Do you choose the lump sum (turn to 44) or the £1,000 a year (turn to 428)? If you think the whole thing is just a load of rubbish, bin it and turn to 186.

460

You can feel the tension all around you as the ref makes sure his assistants are ready. He sets his watch, raises his whistle to his lips and . . . *pheeccceep!* The excited crowd cheers as the ball is kicked for the first time.

The Rules of Matchplay are on page 22, and this is where you'll find all the tables mentioned below. Since it's your first match, this paragraph will take you through the first stage.

Start the game by rolling two dice. If your Midfield Skill is higher than your opponents' Midfield Skill, add **1** to the dice roll; if it's lower, subtract **1**.

Look up your roll on the Open Play Table. What does it tell you to do?

⚽ If it says 'Time + 1', the first 15 minutes has been uneventful. Cross off one of the numbers on the Referee's Watch on Match Sheet 1.

⚽ If it says 'Special', roll two dice and go to the Special Event Table to see what happens.

⚽ If it tells you that one of the teams is attacking, roll two dice and go to the Attack Table. Whoever is attacking, look at that team's Attack Skill. If it's higher than the other team's Defence Skill, add **1** to the dice roll. If it's lower, subtract **1**.

Follow whatever instructions you are given, then go back to the Open Play Table to carry on with the match.

It's easy when you get used to it. Now it's up to you! Keep going according to the rules, remembering to note any goals and special events on your Match Sheet.

When 45 minutes are up, turn to 547.

461

You decide there's to be no let up, and you put your players through a gruelling schedule of tackling, shooting and dribbling practice. Sure, they're fit enough, but unfortunately you've worn them out. Your team will have to start the match tired: lose **1** Morale.

Roll one dice. You may subtract one from your dice roll if you've hired Fiona Turner. If you roll 1–3, turn to 490. If you roll 4–6, turn to 507.

462

Write the names of your team next to their positions (Defender, Midfielder, Attacker) on Match Sheet 1, which you'll find on page 274. Fill in their Skills as well.

Now add up the Skills of all your Defenders to get your Defence Skill. Do the same for your Attack Skill and Midfield Skill. Remember also that you can divide your Morale and Fitness scores as you wish among all three of these Skill scores. When you've done that, write the new totals in the box provided on your Match Sheet.

Finally, this is a Home game: that gives you an advantage in all areas of play, so you may add **1** to each of these totals.

Ready for the big match? Turn to 8.

463

You wince. It's the worst possible outcome. Not only is the card coming from the ref's top pocket a red one, he's pointing to the spot as well.

Roll a dice for each of your defenders in turn. Keep going through the list until you roll a 1; that player has been sent off.

Breathe deeply and gather your dice again as your players gather pointlessly around the ref. Try to ignore the huge cheer from the joyful crowd opposite you; not to mention the half-dozen red flares that have been ignited in the home stand, just for such an occasion. Then roll for this penalty in the usual way. If it's a goal – and let's face it, they usually are – mark it up on the Match Sheet and get on with the game. Remember to cross off the guilty player and adjust your Skill scores accordingly. You can bring on a sub if you want, but only if you bring someone else off – you are down to ten men now!

Turn to 382.

464

Inside is a small tube of fine black powder, a soft brush and a pair of white cotton gloves. They fit perfectly. There is a short information leaflet, explaining how to use the equipment. Stow

this fingerprinting kit in your desk drawer and make a note of it on your Fact Sheet. Then turn to 238.

465

Are you jetlagged or something? Don't be such a mug. These things are a complete load of rubbish! Anyway, don't you earn that sort of money in a week? Get on with doing what you're best at and turn to 186.

466

The bulk of your time this week will be dedicated to improving the skills of your chosen goalkeeper, paying particular attention to aerial reflexes and closing down the angle of attack. Roll two dice. If you roll 9 or more, turn to 398. If 8 or less, turn to 335. If you are employing Hans Gross you may add **2** to your dice roll.

467

You felt scared when you saw the look in Heather's eyes. Now you're terrified. Inside are three black-and-white A4 photographs. One shows Heather standing on the steps of her home. Another shows her helping her two young children into her car. The third is Heather helping the same children out of the car, in front of the school gates. You notice how happy they all look.

Heather has started to cry again. Nigel's face has turned as white as flour.

Blackmail. Someone has been spying on Heather: they know where she lives and where her children go to school.

'Who?' you ask.

'Do you really think I know the answer to that?' Heather asks wearily.

'Then how –' You stop short – there are too many questions. Over the next ten minutes Heather explains how she received the photographs along with an anonymous letter. Another letter soon followed instructing her to put certain players out of action for the cup season. It was up to her how she did it, but if she failed her family would be in danger.

'What was I supposed to do?' she demands, and this time you don't have an answer.

Turn to 21.

468

There is interest in only one of your players this time round, and that's Howie Jevons. If you want to see how much you can get for him, turn to 59. Otherwise go back to 248 and make another choice.

469

You give the iron rod an almighty yank. A long way inside you hear a distant clanging, and a number of big-sounding dogs start barking their heads off. What are you going to do? If you wait and introduce yourself, turn to 534. If you run and hide, turn to 97.

470

'I need to know what you've taken, Salvatore,' you explain firmly. 'Everything.'

He sighs and looks at you with a half smile, as if talking to you is just a pointless game.

'Painkillers, for back. Vitamins. Iron pill. Happy now?'

'That's everything?'

'Oh, and steroid. Silly Salvatore, I nearly forget,' he adds sarcastically.

'You realise how serious this is, don't you?' you ask him.

For the first time he drops his aggressive stare and suddenly looks weak and scared.

'Of course, boss. But I do nothing wrong and now I cannot play. And I don't understand.'

Make a note of anything you'd like to remember from this conversation, and turn to 6.

471

The police arrive within twenty minutes, and Dr McCullough is taken away for questioning. You and Nigel agree that the details of this matter should remain between the two of you for now. If the players find out their own doctor was trying to ruin their careers, there would be an outcry, and you could wave goodbye to the trophy this year. It will come out in the end, of course, but until then you have a job to do. Turn to 537.

472

Do you want to take anyone along with you? You have room for one more in your car. But who can you trust?

If you invite Nigel, turn to 414.

If you invite Heather, turn to 94.

If you go alone, turn to 473.

473

Dusk is falling as you make the hour-long journey to Calverton, and the street lights are beginning to flicker into life. The sun has just dipped behind the horizon and is painting the small, high clouds pink with the last of its light. You watch the faces behind the wheels of the rush-hour cars as they pass, wishing you were one of them, returning through the calm evening to the safety of home.

You turn off the main road and drive a short distance through countryside before the old pit comes into view through the gloom. It's disused now, and the pulley wheel at the top of the stack hasn't turned for many years.

You don't think about it for long. You're entering the western outskirts of the town, and off to the right a large house is looming into view.

Turn to 509.

474

Have you discovered a surname during your investigation? If so, turn to 103. If not, turn to 343.

475

The card flashes an angry crimson as the ref holds it high above his head. Why, you wonder as your shame-faced player trudges from the field, do they make such a song and dance of holding up a card – standing there like a high court judge, sending a condemned man to his doom? Pure theatre. But at least he isn't signalling a penalty. It is, however, a free kick; and right on the edge of the area.

First, roll a dice for each of your defenders in turn. Keep going until you roll a 1; that player has been sent off. Adjust your Defence Skill accordingly and make a note of this dismissal next to that player's name on your Match Sheet. Remember he cannot play in the next match either! Now take the free kick for the opposition in the usual way. Remember to update your Match Sheet if – God forbid – they score.

Now turn to 382.

476

> ### Noordenhaarenijk
> Manager: Dirck Groot
> Formation: 4-4-2
> Defence Skill: 19
> Midfield Skill: 23
> Attack Skill: 21

Make the necessary adjustments to your Match Sheet; the game is ready to kick off. Turn to 61.

477

Bailey is an awkward individual. At home he is fine and fits into the team well, but he is not a good traveller and becomes fussy and restless when away from home. Subtract two points from his Skill for this match only. You don't notice how uncomfortable he is until half-time, so you may not substitute him until then.

Now turn to 331.

478

'Wait. I'm curious,' you say truthfully, before turning to Heather McCullough and speaking in a low voice.

'You've made my life hell for the last three weeks and you may already have ruined this club. But before we report you I want to hear why you went to such lengths to drug three of our players, knowing that if you got caught, your career would be over.'

There is a strangely calm silence before Heather speaks.

'I had no choice,' she whispers, finally raising her gaze to meet your own. She looks exhausted, but there is a defiance in her eyes which scares you. Without another word she places a brown envelope on the desk between you. You realise that you are playing detective again – how typical – and this could land you in trouble with the police when it's time to make your statement. But you're fiercely curious. It's your move: what do you do?

If you are sick of her excuses, push the envelope right back and tell Nigel to get the police over right away (turn to 471). If you need to know, take the envelope and see what's inside (turn to 467).

479

You believe that one of the keys to success is Flexibility. No one wins a race by standing still, and you're ready to change direction as necessity dictates. This excellent quality also rubs off on your players in training as you are keen that they should all be able to play in each other's positions.

At the start of a match, you may instruct a particular player to play in a floating role. This allows you to divide this player's Skill between two areas. For example, an attacker may drop deep and add his Skill to the Midfield Skill as well as the Attack Skill.

But you may only do this for adjacent regions (Defence-Midfield or Midfield-Attack); and if that player is replaced or sent off you lose this advantage. Your Fitness score must also be **4 or more** for this to work!

Make a note of this on your Fact Sheet on page 284, and write 'Flexible' under Manager Qualities.

Got that? Turn to 209.

480

Roll one dice. If you roll 1–4, turn to 525. If you roll 5 or 6, turn to 349.

481

Well, that's just ridiculous. You'd better rehearse in future if you insist on making these speeches. Lose **1** Morale as your players look at each other and wonder if you've lost it. Now send them out to warm up by turning to 37.

482

Hardwick City, you'll be pleased to hear, will go through on the away goals rule (in other words, by the skin of their teeth). Turn to 372.

483

You peel off the tiny circle of backing paper and stick the microphone under the edge of the desk. You push the jack plug into the recorder and set it to record.

'Testing, testing,' you say out loud, feeling a bit stupid, but the instant the microphone picks up your voice the spools of the miniature cassette begin to turn. When you stop, it stops. You rewind the tape and play it back: 'Testing, testing.' Your own voice speaks back at you, stark and mechanical.

You leave the doctor's office as you found it and place the receiving equipment in your own desk drawer. Thanks to this nifty piece of kit, you can have your ears to the grindstone even when you're not around. Now turn to 485.

484

'You had your chance, Dr McCullough,' you tell her, the friendly tone leaving your voice. 'It's over. Nigel, call the police.'

'With pleasure,' your chairman says.

'I knew I couldn't trust you! You idiots,' she protests, but Nigel is already speaking with a sergeant. You look down at your feet, wondering if you did the right thing.

You didn't. Heather resigns immediately, and when the police question her she denies the blackmail altogether. You wonder why she does this, but you never see her again to find out. The police quickly lose interest after this. Four sportsmen taking drugs, a doctor leaving her job; hardly a criminal case to be solved.

The story ends here. Oh, Hardwick get trounced 5–1 on aggregate in the quarters, by the way. In case you were interested.

Turn to 101.

485

You are so exhausted that when you arrive home you fall straight to sleep. But your dreams are confused and tortured, and you wake up at first light without feeling at all rested. Drink some strong coffee and splash your face with cold water to try to clear your head – you have an important meeting this morning.

You stare at your tired reflection in the mirror, and wonder how football ever got this complicated. Turn to 317.

486

Who did you bring with you? Nigel (turn to 283) or Heather (turn to 453)?

487

If you didn't have to play extra time in the quarters, here's how it works.

Two ninety-minute matches weren't enough to separate you and them. That means an extra thirty minutes of football will now be played, and whoever scores the most goals wins the game.

Trouble is, your players have worked hard in the first ninety minutes, and there's a chance some of them have run out of steam. For each player on your team, roll two dice. If you roll 2 or 12, that player is exhausted. You may substitute them within the normal rules of the game; if you don't, each exhausted player must lose 1 point of Skill for the first 15 minutes and a further point for the second 15 minutes.

Of course if you wish to make any other substitutions you may do that too.

One more thing: do you have the Inspirational managerial quality? If you do, remember this gives you special bonuses in extra time (turn to 455 for a reminder).

When you've finished making adjustments to your team, make them feel good about themselves and send them once more unto the breach. Play just two 15-minute segments. Then turn to 3.

488

The back page of one of the British tabloids is face-up and the headline reads, 'Playing Hard-wick to Get'. It's a rubbish pun even by their standards, but there's no mistaking the tone of the story:

Yesterday, manager of Hardwick City was unavailable for comment on the red hot scandal of the Hardwick Three.

This sentence accompanies a close-up photograph of the palm of your hand as you stride past to avoid the hacks. The article is nothing short of a personal attack on you, and it ends:

Clearly this individual has something to hide. Come on boss! What are you covering up?

This is scandalous! What are they suggesting? That you had something to do with this? But your blood turns cold when you realise that your players are bound to get wind of this before tonight's kick-off, and there's nothing you can do about it. Such is the power of the media: news changes views, whether it's true or not.

Lose **3** Morale. Such vicious rumours about the manager will seriously damage the team spirit. Now turn to 426.

489

TEAM PROFILE
Noordenhaarenijk
Holland

Dutch club football is sometimes perilously ignored by fans over here. True, it's seen more exciting times, but here is a team which can take on any other and teach them a few lessons in technique and professionalism. Their manager puts great emphasis on keeping possession, and these players can pass the ball around the park all day until the opposition get tired or make a silly mistake. Then the strikers are waiting to pounce. Noordenhaarenijk are a fit and powerful unit and Hardwick will need to be equal to them to succeed tonight.

Star Player: Abdou Mbaye
Anchorman

Abdou was born in Senegal but moved to Holland as a teenager. By the time he was fifteen he was already 6'4" and 14 stone, and before long a sharp-eyed local coach spotted his talent and tried him in the centre's role. Mbaye slotted in naturally,

ABDOU MBAYE

combining the quick-stepping African game with his bulk, which can withstand any tackle. In Holland the Noordenhaarenijk fans call him De Boom – 'The Tree' – which is pretty intimidating when it's being chanted by 40,000 of them.

Turn to 155.

490

Normally you would allow the press some access at this time, but you know the question on every journalist's lips today will be about the drug tests. That's the last thing the players need, so you issue a press statement to the effect of 'business as usual'. You can deal with them properly once the match is out of the way.

Hold on – *out of the way*? This is one of the biggest football matches of your career! With three of your best players out of action, it's easy to forget just how much you relish occasions like this. Time to pick your team. Remember, you'll need to choose a goalkeeper, plus ten other players from your squad. Choose a balance of Defenders, Midfielders and Attackers (you **must** choose at least two of each). You'll probably just want to pick the ones with the best Skill scores, but you should also keep an eye on which players combine well together on the pitch.

Done that? Turn to 462.

491

There is some basic medical equipment – a stethoscope, a box of disposable gloves – and assorted stationery. There is a catalogue as well, entitled *Athletics Direct*. Do you look through the catalogue (turn to 221), close the drawer and try the filing cabinet (turn to 23), or leave (turn to 320)?

492

You've obviously been paying attention. This Swedish outfit is renowned for its strong midfield presence, and fire must be met with fire in the centre of the pitch. If their passing is good, yours must be excellent; if they hang on to the ball, you have to hang on tighter. And if you can perfect those through-balls through the gaps, you might just catch them on the hop.

Add **3** to your Midfield score for this match only, as your centres respond well to your efforts. Now turn to 102.

493

You decide to forget the boxes you came in for. They're irrelevant compared to your life. You try to make a break for the ladder, but the flames are fiercer by the second and you are beaten back. You retreat to your corner, the only one that isn't on fire yet.

It's the smoke that kills you. But the flames get you in the end, and your body is never found. Everyone assumes you were to blame for Hardwick's troubles and that you have run away, especially after your earlier encounter with Dr McCullough.

No one ever suspects her. Turn to 101.

494

That sounds about right. Roll one dice: if you roll 4–6 you may add **1** Morale for a decent speech. Add **1** to your roll if you have the Inspirational quality. Now send your players out to warm up by turning to 37.

495

The squad as a whole responds well to your plan. Add **1** to Fitness; and you now have **2** points which you may divide as you wish between your Defence, Midfield and Attack Skills for the next **two** matches only. For example, you may wish to add 1 to your Midfield and 1 to your Defence. Note that this does not permanently increase the skill of any of your players.

Make a note of that on your next two Match Sheets and turn to 278.

496

Zaki's celebration is short. The touch judge is waving his orange and yellow flag wildly, and forty thousand locals suddenly want to buy him a drink. Your heart sinks, but when you see the replay later you have to admit it's tight, but he's right. Roberts' pace got the better of him and he was through the offside trap before Bostock had time to pass the ball back to him. The defenders look more relieved than anything; they know it was a good move and it nearly beat them. At least your team will shortly go into half-time break knowing it was this close, and you may add **1** Morale for that feeling.

Turn to 402.

497

They introduce themselves as before, and almost immediately the draw is underway. The man with glasses whose name you can honestly never remember reaches under the black cloth and into the bowl where the snooker balls are. He swirls them around to make the most of the occasion, and presently pulls one out.

'The first home team will be,' he says slowly, and you could hear a pin drop in the silent boardroom, 'number . . .'

Roll one dice. If you roll 1–3, turn to 109. If you roll 4–6, turn to 135.

498

The atmosphere in the stadium is crackling with anticipation as the shrill shriek of the referee's whistle cuts through the air. The capacity crowd of seventy-five thousand roar as Homens da Guerra kick the game off.

The match couldn't have started better in your dreams. Ben Parker is hacked down by a Portuguese midfielder on the halfway line, and Klaus Wehnert takes the free kick from wide on the right, lofting it over the heads of the players bunched on the edge of the box. It falls to Jed Stevens, who has broken loose on the left, and he runs it along the touch line, past one defender and to the edge of the box, gluing the goalkeeper to his near post. He slots it diagonally across the face of goal, past Danny Knox who dummies and takes another defender out of the equation, and into the path of Duce. The striker has anticipated the move perfectly and ducks away from his marker, sliding in and guiding the ball into the net just inside the right post.

In all your years of club football you've never heard such a bellow from the crowd as you hear now. You stand up and applaud your team as they celebrate, urging them to ride the advantage.

Ten minutes later there's something else for the fans to get excited about. Will Frost is involved in a fifty-fifty collision with a Portuguese midfielder in the centre of the park, and both fall to the ground. Will gets up and play is waved on, but the opposition centre was obviously looking for the free kick and, in his frustration, lashes his foot out at Frost. The linesman waves his flag frantically, and this time the referee stops play. After a short conversation the man in black beckons over the player with a practised index finger and reaches into his pocket.

The card he brings out is red, and every Homens da Guerra

player (even the goalie) crowds round to protest. Why do they bother doing that? Have you ever seen a ref change his mind? The foolish player trudges off the field and the game is restarted with the opposition down to ten men.

But then, as so often happens in these situations, the game changes. No one really knows why ten-men teams suddenly start playing proper football. Some say it's because the remaining players have to throw everything they have at the game; others say it's because it changes the shape of the team and that upsets the opposition. Sometimes you wonder about starting a match with ten just to see what happens, but it's happening in front of you now.

Suddenly Hardwick are in disarray, failing to collect passes and being out-manoeuvred all over midfield. By the time the clock ticks past thirty minutes a sloppy clearance from a corner puts the ball in the middle of the pack. No one quite seems to know where the ball is until the centre-forward manages to toe-poke it past Jamie Coates who is stranded on the goal line. A muck-and-nettles goal, but they all count. One-all.

It goes from bad to worse. Minutes before the half-time whistle, the lone Portuguese striker looks like he's going to cross from the right but instead makes a run into the box. The move catches Carlos de Carvalho off his guard and he sticks a stray foot into the striker's path. The man goes tumbling over and the referee points to the spot.

For the first time ever, you actually don't watch. But when the roar goes up from the Portuguese fans on your left you know exactly what's happened, and seconds after the restart the whistle goes for half-time.

Turn to 286.

499

Pick one player to pay special attention to this week. It's the first leg of the quarters: who is the key to your game plan? When you have chosen someone, turn to 412.

500

'I was just about to tell you,' you are saying.

No wonder the tape's finished, it's picked up the conversation you had with Heather and Nigel after the semi-final draw. But how?

Your head is swimming with the impossibility of it all. What do you do?

Search your office for bugs?   (Turn to 240)
Listen to the whole of the tape again?   (Turn to 148)

501

Score 2 points for your answer. Jot this down somewhere on your Fact Sheet (page 284) – you'll need to refer to it later. Now turn to 128.

502

Competition rules limit the number of players that may be added to your squad once the tournament has begun. So you may choose only one of the following to add to your squad:

Calum Doughty (Reserves)
Position: Defender (Skill 5)
Age: 26

Dave Honess (Reserves)
Position: Midfielder (Skill 5)
Age: 24

Paul Price (Youth team)
Position: Attacker (Skill 5)
Age: 16

Make your decision, and write your new player's name and Skill on your Squad Details on page 285. When you've done that, turn to 312.

503

You have chosen the skill of Diplomacy. Football managers some-times seem to be all mouth and ego, but you're the exception: expert communicators like you are particularly good at seeing ways through tricky situations. You're also a model of cool when you give one of your famous talks. Diplomacy will be particularly useful when you are negotiating to buy a new player to add to your squad. You will be given special instructions when this happens. For now, just write 'Diplomatic' under Manager Qualities on your Fact Sheet (page 284). When you've done that you may turn to 209.

504

The heavy red can lies at your feet, and you heave it upright. With a sharp tug you pull out the pin and throw it aside. You angle the horn so it is pointing at the sacks and boxes that the fire is feast-ing on, and squeeze the trigger hard. There is a rush of white gas which engulfs the burning debris and for a few seconds you can't see anything. As it clears you see that the sack is still smouldering, but the flames have gone! You turn the jet on the next sack, and the next, until the canister is empty and only lazy wisps of smoke remain.

But what's this? You're breathing, but it's like you're holding your breath. You gulp faster and faster breaths, but you're suffocating – you've filled the small chamber with deadly carbon dioxide, and there's no oxygen left. Spots start to dance before your eyes . . .

You grab the boxes you came in for, and with your remaining strength you haul yourself up the ladder to the ledge, grasping for the handle of the metal door between you and the outside world.

Did you take the padlock? If you did, turn to 48. If not, turn to 229.

505

The player is with Real Sabadell, and he has been ruled out for six weeks with a calf strain. Shame – unless Real Sabadell are your opposition tomorrow. If they are, turn to 409. If not, kill time by doing a few puzzles from your *Sudoku Genius* book until you arrive at your destination. Then turn to 355.

506

Thursday 16th

You're one match into the competition. Hopefully you managed to put other matters out of your mind during the football, but you're in charge of a club in crisis. The press are clamouring to see you, and you know from experience that the longer you leave them the noisier they get. You refused the customary post-match interview last night; but best not keep them out much longer or the rumour mill will start grinding out the usual stories, and they're always much worse than the truth.

That nagging voice again. What *is* the truth? You haven't spoken to any of the players since Monday, when it all happened. You've got the place pretty much to yourself for the next four hours until the team arrives for training. That gives you plenty of time to talk to the three players who tested positive, if you wish.

If that's what you'd like to do, turn to 310. If you'd rather forget all about them, turn to 332.

507

It gets worse: all your slave-driving means one of your players got flattened in a tackle and has suffered a groin strain. Roll one dice to see whose groin it was.

1   Jamie Coates

2   Carlos de Carvalho
3   Dmitri Duval
4   John Hoggart
5   Ian Leslie
6   Jed Stevens

That player is injured and will not have time to recover before the match.

Now turn to 490.

508

A cheer goes up from your players' table when you walk into the bar, and they fall over themselves to buy you a drink.

'Thought you were going to stand us up, chief!' Jamie Coates says.

'I would very like to say, thank you for being a manager *par excellence*, and . . . and . . . we love you.' Dmitri Duval has had one drink too many and looks a little offended as the other players jeer him.

You congratulate them on their performances to get this far, but remind them that there is a long way to go before they can kiss the trophy. Then you tell them the good news.

'I have pleasure in informing you,' you say with a genuine grin, 'that there were no further positive results today. All six players tested negative so I think we can safely say we're at full strength.'

'Of course,' Dmitri Duval says. 'I never do drug.'

'Mein Gott,' Klaus Wehnert says, taking a long swig of his beer. 'I hope that's the last time for me.'

But you are looking at Steve, and Steve is staring into space, with a look on his face that is half panic, half bewilderment. You know what he's been up to, but he doesn't know you know. And that

means – as long as you're careful – you're holding all the cards.
Turn to 511.

509

You decide it's too risky to take the car up the crunching gravel of the drive, so you park by a hedge at the bottom of the hill, out of sight. You lock the car and stand facing the house on the hill.

Are you alone (turn to 54) or with a companion (turn to 361)?

510

'Since we're having such a nice chat,' Greg says, 'why don't we make it a real party?' He presses the button on a silver intercom panel fixed to the wall. 'Darling,' he says, 'why don't you come and join us?'

After a few moments the door behind you opens, and a woman steps into the room.

It's Dr McCullough. Turn to 173.

511

Thursday 30th

The following morning you allow yourself a short lie-in. The players won't be turning up at the club until around eleven, when the draw for the quarter-finals will be made at UEFA headquarters on the shores of Lake Geneva. You are first in the boardroom, where the table has been removed to make way for more seats, and a live satellite feed has been set up by the club technicians. You know that seven other managers across Europe will be gathering their squads for this event, and although the draw only takes a few minutes it always has a special buzz. The papers are full of speculation about who Hardwick will be drawn against, which teams might be the easiest to beat and which the hardest. You don't really care, since any team will pose a challenge at this stage.

One by one the players turn up and take their places. By ten to eleven the room is packed: as well as the players, all of the ground staff, admin workers and executives are here too, and there is standing room only.

The projector is switched on and the screen flickers into life. You see the familiar faces of the UEFA chief executive and chairman, standing behind a counter into which is set a large bowl, covered with black cloth. They are grinning like a pair of schoolkids who have just been picked to be team mascots.

'A warm welcome to all our viewers, players and managers around Europe for the live draw for the quarter-finals of the UEFA European Cup,' one says to the camera, eyes flashing excitedly from behind wire-framed spectacles. 'Only eight teams are now remaining in the competition, and we wish them all the best of luck.'

'Get on with it,' shouts Jed Stevens, and several other players tell him to shut up.

'I will draw the home teams,' the official continues, 'beginning with . . .'

There is stony silence in the room as he reaches under the cloth and pulls out a white snooker ball with a number painted on the side.

'Number six,' he announces, placing the ball on a small plastic stand. 'Kött Fotbollar, from Sweden!'

The other man reaches into the bowl and draws the next ball.

'And they will host . . .' He peers from behind his wire-framed glasses at the number on the ball. 'Number one: Lazzaro di Savena, from Italy.'

The ball is placed next to the first on the stand. Three matches to go.

The third ball is drawn from under the cloth and the announcement is made.

'Number four. Hardwick City, from the United Kingdom!' Your heart leaps, and several people in the room shift nervously on their seats as the next ball is drawn.

'And they will be at home to . . .'

Roll one dice.

If you roll 1 or 6, turn to 177.

If you roll 2 or 5, turn to 541.

If you roll 3 or 4, turn to 550.

512

Where can you place a single microphone when you don't even know who you're trying to bug? But then a thought occurs to you. Where would you go in a busy building if you wanted privacy?

You walk to the men's room and are glad to see the cleaners have already been in. You find a spot under the U-bend that is still a bit dusty and tape the bug to it – obviously they don't clean there, it should be safe.

Now turn to 537.

513

Turn to 434.

514

Turn to 296.

515

Fiona Turner has joined the club on a six-month contract. You're lucky! Fiona is a bright, perceptive sports-injury expert. Aches and pains, breaks and sprains, she knows her onions. There are two benefits to having Fiona working for you. First, you may add **1** to your Fitness straight away. And second, you may subtract **1** from your dice roll whenever you roll to see if an injured player has recovered before a match. Make a note of these benefits under Management Information on your Fact Sheet on page 284, and remember to write down 'Fiona Turner, Physiotherapist' as well.

Done that? Turn to 480.

516

Are you ready to get on with it yet? If you've finished your emergency reshuffle, turn to 271. If you want to look at your staffing situation, turn to 252. If you want to address your own personal management qualities, turn to 184.

517

You all board the aircraft together and take your seats in First Class. Once airborne the deep growl of the engines soon sends you to sleep, and you awake as you are touching down in Germany.

Turn to 294.

518

You have chosen to be a Tactician. This means you are an expert in seeing how a particular player's qualities could change the course of a match. Whenever you bring on a substitute at half time or during the second half of a match, that player becomes a Supersub and you may add **2** to his Skill.

Important: You may only do this for one sub per match, and it only lasts for the duration of that match.

Important: Being Tactical means you may not choose the quality Instinctive.

Write 'Tactical' on your Fact Sheet under Manager Qualities, make a note of the special advantage it gives you and turn to 209.

519

The three of you gather eagerly around your computer and type the name Greg Ventner into a search engine. Within a second a page comes up, showing several hits. The first hit is a red herring, just a misprint of someone else's name. The rest are rather more interesting. Click on one and turn to 45.

520

You know that if you hesitate you run the risk of being spotted by someone else, or worse, by Steve himself. Feeling like a criminal, you reach over and quickly, silently pluck the phone from the pocket of the sleepy oaf. His big head lolls to one side and he blows a raspberry through his lips like a donkey.

You sit for a few seconds, motionless, making sure Steve is still asleep.

Then his eyes flick open, and he looks straight at you.

'What the hell are you doing?' he says.

Turn to 257.

521

The European Cup schedule is a punishing one, and your match against the German side Bayern Badetuch is next Tuesday evening. It's an away match, which means travelling the night before – that only makes four days available for training. You can hear your players arriving and greeting each other, and you need to decide how you are going to spend this time. What do your plans involve?

Heavy fitness work followed by a training match?

(Turn to 69)

Individual skills, light fitness and tactics? (Turn to 125)

Socialising and watching your favourite football videos?

(Turn to 142)

522

It takes a bit of research, but eventually you are able to track down a mysterious woman who goes by the name of Charlotte-Ann. Maybe mystics are like Brazilians and only need a first name. You're a bit dismayed by the fact that she went to the wrong address at first, but during the interview she assures you that she is 'Britain's leading psychic' and you're sold on her claim to have special powers to influence the decisions of match officials or produce spectacular improvements in a player's performance.

In this book, if you ever need to call on her psychic abilities during a match or during training, turn to 208 and you will be given special instructions. But you may only do this once during the whole book. It's your picnic! Write this down alongside 'Charlotte-Ann, Psychic' under Management Information on your Fact Sheet (page 284). Now turn to 480.

523

You are so exhausted that when you arrive home you fall straight to sleep. But your dreams are confused and tortured, and you wake up at first light without feeling at all rested. Drink some strong coffee and splash your face in cold water to try to clear your head – you have an important meeting this morning.

You stare at your tired reflection in the mirror, and wonder how football ever got this complicated. Turn to 545.

524

Notebooks are pulled out and cameras held high as you push open one of the large double doors and enter the boardroom. You smile and nod at a couple of familiar faces in the crowd before taking your seat at the front, behind a long trestle table draped with Hardwick's colours.

'Thanks for coming,' you tell the eager journalists. 'Ready when you are.'

A dozen hands shoot up and you pick one at random. It belongs to a skinny young man with a blotchy face like a ripe peach.

'Frank Seely, *Evening Post.* Can you sum up tonight's game for us, please?'

'I see you're going to make me do all the work, then,' you reply with a grin. But what will you say?

'I'm on top of the moon. Tonight's result has left us well ahead for Friday's return leg and I can only look forward to it now.'

(Turn to 203)

'We had some boys on there tonight and I asked them to do a man's job. We tried to sit back and defend for ninety minutes, and you can't do that at this level.' (Turn to 528)

'It's natural at this level to defend deep and hang on to what you've got, but I'll not apologise because we're right in the cart.'

(Turn to 34)

525

That's your staff situation dealt with. What else do you want to do?

Consider your own managerial strengths? (Turn to 184)
Look at your reserve team? (Turn to 74)
Forget all that and get on with the football? (Turn to 271)

526
Impossible. You have no evidence that all three players took that particular substance. You turn your mind back to your conversations with them. Turn to 68.

527
Wednesday passes uneventfully, with the team sticking to their original training plan. On Thursday afternoon you and the players congregate on the team coach and are driven to the airport for your away match tomorrow night.

As the plane takes off, you take off your shoes and catch up with the sports news. One story catches your eye: it's about an injury to a key player from – which team is that? Roll one dice while you get your reading glasses out.

If you roll 1 or 2, turn to 551.

If you roll 3 or 4, turn to 407.

If you roll 5 or 6, turn to 505.

528
If you lost tonight, or drew with two or more goals scored against you, turn to 227. Otherwise turn to 111.

529
There in front of you is your cassette recorder. Twenty-four hours earlier it had been wound right back to the start – you'd checked. Now there is a thin band of black tape clearly showing at one end.

The bug in the men's room must have picked something up!

You try to remain calm, tell yourself it could be anything – but those mikes only pick up voices, and why would anyone be talking in a lavatory cubicle unless they had something to hide?

You rewind the tape and click play. You are immediately disappointed as you hear the voice of one of the groundsmen bemoaning his job and talking to someone on the phone about packing it in. But that only lasts half a minute, and there is tape to spare. A low hiss, the stop-start *clickclick* of the machine, then this:

'Greg? It's me.'

It's a voice you know, but can't place yet.

'Yeah. No. Don't think so.'

There's no mistaking that. It's Steve Fitzgerald. He's a man of few words, and you hope he's not thinking of resigning as well. But wait: there's more.

'I did what you said and took the steroids meself this time. Tip off the labs and I'll be the next to get the push, definite. No one will suspect us after that – we'll be home and dry. OK. OK. Cheers.'

Your blood is pounding in your ears and you replay the recording to make sure you didn't miss anything. It's Steve all right. But who is this Greg? You run through names in your head but don't believe you've ever known a Greg. It's no one who works here.

Make a note of what you've heard and turn to 133.

530

Do you want to investigate the incinerator (turn to 309), or do you think it would be better to wait for Nigel Douglas to arrive and explain the truth (turn to 340)? If you leave your office, you may take one item with you if you wish. Make your choice from the picture below and make a note of what you've taken on your Fact Sheet.

531

As a result of your work, one of your players has achieved a new level of skill. Pick up a pencil and turn to your Squad Details. Now close your eyes and pick a player at random. You may add **1** to this player's Skill.

Ready? Turn to 411.

532

How much money will Voss command on the transfer market? Here's how to find out. Roll one dice and subtract it from his Skill. This is the amount, in millions, that you are being offered. (Add 1 to this number if you have the Diplomatic Quality as you are very persuasive.) If you accept the money, add it to your Budget and cross off Barry from your Squad Details (page 285). Or you may refuse the offer if you wish. When you're ready, turn back to 250 for more big business options.

533

Nigel suggests you take the right flight. Turn to 367.

534

A man in a cap opens the door. He is gripping a short leather leash at the end of which is a three-headed Alsatian — no, wait — *three* Alsatians, all craning their necks around to see what you might taste like.

You introduce yourself, and the man smiles on one side of his mouth.

'You'd better come in,' he says. It's the last thing you do. Something heavy and hard comes down on the back of your neck as you step into the hall, and the lights go out.

Turn to 101.

535

You managed to stop them scoring a single goal on their home ground! They'll be annoyed about that. Congratulate your defenders on such sterling work, and turn to 89 to record this result in the Group Table.

536

If you're hosting Liblonec Vyoslav, turn to 16. If Lazzaro di Savena are your opponents, turn to 58.

537

Wednesday 22nd, 10 a.m.

You gather your team in the dressing room: it's time to take stock. Perhaps you've already secured your place in the quarter-finals, perhaps there's still all to play for; either way, you've a match you must play in a week's time against Kött Fotbollar, the current kings of Swedish football.

'We're two games into the group stage, and only the cream of the crop get further than this,' you tell your team. 'Kött are already through to the next round, but that doesn't mean they'll be a pushover. In fact, they'll be relaxed and that could make them even more dangerous.'

'What's Kött?' Jed Stevens asks. He looks confused.

'The team we're playing next week,' you remind him. 'From Sweden.'

'Where's Sweden?'

There are whoops of laughter as the other players realise that Jed actually hasn't heard of Sweden.

You consider your options as you wait for the laughter to die down and Jed to stop blushing. This will be a home match, so at least you have that advantage. But perhaps you already know something about the way your Swedish opponents play. What special measures could you take to ensure victory?

If you want to concentrate on your defence, turn to 282.

If you prefer to work on your midfield, turn to 492.

If you think the key is in a strong attack, turn to 333.

538

It's clear as soon as you begin to work with Aspachs that communication is going to be a problem here. Without an interpreter to help him through the language barrier he quickly becomes isolated and unhappy. He will still play for you, but with a reduced Skill of only **5**.

Make the adjustment to your Squad Details and turn back to 250.

539

Look back over the results so far. Put the team with the best Goal Difference first. If two teams have the same Goal Difference, turn to 432. If the table is now complete, turn to 139.

540

Hmm. Suppose that just about makes sense, for a football manager. Your players seem convinced and ready to go. Send them out to warm up by turning to 37.

541

'Number eight. Noordenhaarenijk, from Holland!'

You've never actually seen Noordenhaarenijk play live, but you are familiar with many of their players from televised matches. One of them, Joe Fry, used to play for you before manager Dirck Groot made you an offer you couldn't refuse.

You'll have a chance to find out more about your opponents later. Until then, make a note of this fixture on your next two Match Sheets, then turn to 380.

542

Well, that explains a lot: why Steve Fitzgerald has been in such close contact with Greg; and why Greg seems to have such power over him, even when Steve's own very successful career is at stake. But it raises more questions. Why did Greg Ventner's own career disappear without trace? Many footballers successfully return to top flight football after accidents. And why is he still so desperate to bring failure to Hardwick?

'We could tell the police now,' Nigel offers. 'Now we know all this.'

But Heather disagrees.

'A few articles on the Internet? Where's the proof?'

Not for the first time in these last weeks the two of them look to you for good ideas. And not for the first time, you don't feel you have any.

Turn to 225.

543

That's the end of the football season for Hardwick. The media pressure is off, but it looks like the drugs did their job: you're out of this competition, and the book. Turn to 101.

544

'It's, just, erm,' you falter, pushing papers round on your desk nervously. Steve is waiting patiently. Quick! Think of something! 'They've got a new rule, no coffee within an hour of the samples being taken.'

'No coffee?'

'No. Or tea.'

'No coffee or tea?'

'That's right. It mucks up the testosterone count. Apparently. Can you let everyone know please?' You smile hopefully.

Steve nods briskly and ducks out of your office. That was rubbish! Be more careful in future or all your hard work will have been wasted.

You may now interview Dr McCullough if you wish, by turning to 194. If you'd prefer to get on with preparations for the match tonight, turn to 327.

545

Wednesday 22nd, 7 a.m.

Your heart is pounding as you drive your sports car past security and park in your reserved space. You are here earlier than usual, so when you reach the bottom of the basement stairs you are not surprised to see that the lights in Heather's office are still off. That means she hasn't arrived yet. It's only seven thirty, and she normally starts work at around eight. You go in and wait for her – you wanted the advantage of surprise, and you've got it. But only just: the door behind you is opening, and the lights have been turned on. Heather has arrived early: turn to 444.

546

You try to access Greg's number, but it is listed as name only. The number has been encrypted and is accessible only by password. Better not hang around guessing – Steve could wake up at any moment.

If you want to search for text messages, turn to 86. Otherwise turn to 318.

547

How's the game going? Is your team:

Winning?   (Turn to 552)
Drawing or losing? (Turn to 202)

548

Hallelujah! You're at the top of the table with six points already, alongside the Swedes. Both other teams are out already, which means Hardwick City and Kött Fotbollar both progress to the second round! But there's still the matter of which of you comes top of your group, and that's worth it for the prestige alone.

Yes, yes, you're great. Now get on with it by turning to 218.

549

Huh? The ref is pointing, but it's not to the penalty spot as you'd hoped. He's judged that the goalkeeper did nothing wrong, and he's signalling a goal kick! You can't believe it any more than the Hardwick fans can, and they are roundly booing the man in black. Somehow you don't think he'll be going out in Hardwick tonight.

Still, your players know that Stevens and Bostock did well to force such risky play from the goalkeeper and you may add **1** Morale.

Now turn to 304.

550

'Number two. Cochons d'Inde, from France!'

Cochons d'Inde have let in fewer goals so far in this competition than any other team, and they will be a hard nut to crack.

You'll be able to read more about this team later. For now, make a note of this fixture on your next two Match Sheets; then turn to 380.

551

It's Noordenhaarenijk, and they have lost an important member of their team to cruciate ligament damage in training. Are they your opponents tomorrow? If so, turn to 409. If not, pore over the rest of the news until you touch down at your destination (turn to 355).

552

You've obviously got the measure of these opponents, but beware:

this game isn't over yet. Let your guard down in the second half and things could change in the blink of an eye. If you want to make any half-time substitutions, do it now (remember you may bring on up to three substitutes in one game). You might want to give other team members a chance on the field, perhaps to keep your best players free from injury. Or, if Hardwick has pulled ahead by a significant number of goals, you might want to make tactical substitutions to replace Attackers with Midfielders or Defenders. This will make it harder for you to score more goals, but easier to stop Revolyutsiya scoring!

Whatever you do will change the course of the game, so remember to update the Skill scores on your Match Sheet if you make any changes.

Now turn to 228.

Turn the page for paragraph 553 . .

Hardwick City 3 – 2 Homens da Guerra

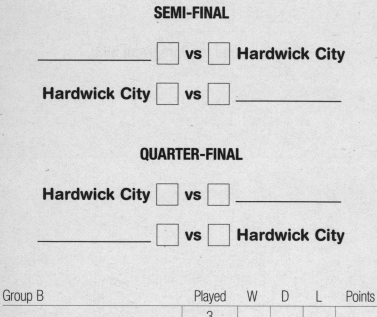

SEMI-FINAL

_____ ☐ vs ☐ Hardwick City

Hardwick City ☐ vs ☐ _____

QUARTER-FINAL

Hardwick City ☐ vs ☐ _____

_____ ☐ vs ☐ Hardwick City

Group B	Played	W	D	L	Points
	3				
	3				
	3				
	3				

You've won the European Cup!

Match Sheet 1: Wednesday 15th

Hardwick City ☐ vs ☐ Revolyutsiya Apelsyn

Team Selection

No.	Position	Player name	Skill	Injuries, cards
2	Goalkeeper			
3	Defender			
4	Defender			
5	Def/Mid			
6	Def/Mid			
7	Midfielder			
8	Midfielder			
9	Mid/Att			
10	Mid/Att			
11	Attacker			
12	Attacker			

NB subtract 2 from the Skill of any player playing outside his normal position for this match.

Hardwick

Defence Skill ☐

Midfield Skill ☐

Attack Skill ☐

Revolyutsiya

☐ Attack Skill

☐ Midfield Skill

☐ Defence Skill

Add 1 to each of your Skill totals if you're playing a home game, otherwise subtract 1. You may split your Morale and Fitness among your Skill scores however you wish.

Referee's Watch	15	30	45	60	75	90

Substitutes & Scorers

. . . .

. . . .

. . . .

. . . .

. . . .

Match Sheet 2: Tuesday 21st

Bayern Badetuch ☐ vs ☐ Hardwick City

Team Selection

No.	Position	Player name	Skill	Injuries, cards
2	Goalkeeper			
3	Defender			
4	Defender			
5	Def/Mid			
6	Def/Mid			
7	Midfielder			
8	Midfielder			
9	Mid/Att			
10	Mid/Att			
11	Attacker			
12	Attacker			

NB subtract 2 from the Skill of any player playing outside his normal position for this match.

Bayern Badetuch

Defence Skill ☐
Midfield Skill ☐
Attack Skill ☐

Hardwick City

☐ Attack Skill
☐ Midfield Skill
☐ Defence Skill

Add 1 to each of your Skill totals if you're playing a home game, otherwise subtract 1. You may split your Morale and Fitness among your Skill scores however you wish.

Referee's Watch

15	30	45	60	75	90

Substitutes & Scorers

Match Sheet 3: Wednesday 29th

Hardwick City ☐ vs ☐ Kött Fotbollar

Team Selection

No.	Position	Player name	Skill	Injuries, cards
2	Goalkeeper			
3	Defender			
4	Defender			
5	Def/Mid			
6	Def/Mid			
7	Midfielder			
8	Midfielder			
9	Mid/Att			
10	Mid/Att			
11	Attacker			
12	Attacker			

NB subtract 2 from the Skill of any player playing outside his normal position for this match.

Hardwick

Defence Skill ☐

Midfield Skill ☐

Attack Skill ☐

Kött Fotbollar

☐ Attack Skill

☐ Midfield Skill

☐ Defence Skill

Add 1 to each of your Skill totals if you're playing a home game, otherwise subtract 1. You may split your Morale and Fitness among your Skill scores however you wish.

Referee's Watch

15	30	45	60	75	90

Substitutes & Scorers

. . . .
. . . .
. . . .
. . . .
. . . .

Final Group Standings

The top two teams from each group go through to the quarter-final draw.

Group A	Played	W	D	L	Points
Homens da Guerra (Por)	3	3	0	0	9
Liblonec Vyoslav (Cze)	3	1	1	1	4
Neftyanye Oligarhi (Rus)	3	1	0	2	3
Balbeg Rangers (Sco)	3	0	1	2	1

Group B	Played	W	D	L	Points
	3				
	3				
	3				
	3				

NB transfer Group B results here from paragraph 120 if you want to see the whole picture

Group C	Played	W	D	L	Points
Lazzaro di Savena (Ita)	3	2	1	0	7
Cochons d'Inde (Fra)	3	2	0	1	6
Badamancia (Spa)	3	1	1	1	4
FC Sklavenitis (Gre)	3	0	0	3	0

Group D	Played	W	D	L	Points
Noordenhaarenijk (Hol)	3	2	0	1	6
Real Sabadell (Spa)	3	1	2	0	5
AC Catarugia (Ita)	3	1	1	1	4
Fenersikaray (Tur)	3	0	1	2	1

Match Sheet 4: Tuesday 4th
Quarter Final (first leg)

Hardwick City ☐ vs ☐ _____

Team Selection

No.	Position	Player name	Skill	Injuries, cards
2	Goalkeeper			
3	Defender			
4	Defender			
5	Def/Mid			
6	Def/Mid			
7	Midfielder			
8	Midfielder			
9	Mid/Att			
10	Mid/Att			
11	Attacker			
12	Attacker			

NB subtract 2 from the Skill of any player playing outside his normal position for this match.

Hardwick		**Opponents**	
Defence Skill	☐	☐	Attack Skill
Midfield Skill	☐	☐	Midfield Skill
Attack Skill	☐	☐	Defence Skill

Add 1 to each of your Skill totals if you're playing a home game, otherwise subtract 1. You may split your Morale and Fitness among your Skill scores however you wish.

Referee's Watch

15	30	45	60	75	90

Substitutes & Scorers

....
....
....
....

Match Sheet 5: Friday 7th
Quarter Final (second leg)

_____ ☐ vs ☐ **Hardwick City**

Team Selection

No.	Position	Player name	Skill	Injuries, cards
2	Goalkeeper			
3	Defender			
4	Defender			
5	Def/Mid			
6	Def/Mid			
7	Midfielder			
8	Midfielder			
9	Mid/Att			
10	Mid/Att			
11	Attacker			
12	Attacker			

NB subtract 2 from the Skill of any player playing outside his normal position for this match.

Hardwick

Defence Skill ☐

Midfield Skill ☐

Attack Skill ☐

Opponents

☐ Attack Skill

☐ Midfield Skill

☐ Defence Skill

Add 1 to each of your Skill totals if you're playing a home game, otherwise subtract 1. You may split your Morale and Fitness among your Skill scores however you wish.

Referee's Watch	15	30	45	60	75	90

Substitutes & Scorers

....
....
....
....

Match Sheet 6: Tuesday 11th
Semi-final (first leg)

_____ [ ] vs [ ] **Hardwick City**

Team Selection

No.	Position	Player name	Skill	Injuries, cards
2	Goalkeeper			
3	Defender			
4	Defender			
5	Def/Mid			
6	Def/Mid			
7	Midfielder			
8	Midfielder			
9	Mid/Att			
10	Mid/Att			
11	Attacker			
12	Attacker			

NB subtract 2 from the Skill of any player playing outside his normal position for this match.

Hardwick
Defence Skill [ ]
Midfield Skill [ ]
Attack Skill [ ]

Opponents
[ ] Attack Skill
[ ] Midfield Skill
[ ] Defence Skill

Add 1 to each of your Skill totals if you're playing a home game, otherwise subtract 1. You may split your Morale and Fitness among your Skill scores however you wish.

Referee's Watch | 15 | 30 | 45 | 60 | 75 | 90 |

Substitutes & Scorers

. . . .
. . . .
. . . .
. . . .

Match Sheet 7: Friday 14th
Semi-final (second leg)

Hardwick City [ ] vs [ ] _____

Team Selection

No.	Position	Player name	Skill	Injuries, cards
2	Goalkeeper			
3	Defender			
4	Defender			
5	Def/Mid			
6	Def/Mid			
7	Midfielder			
8	Midfielder			
9	Mid/Att			
10	Mid/Att			
11	Attacker			
12	Attacker			

NB subtract 2 from the Skill of any player playing outside his normal position for this match.

Hardwick
Defence Skill [ ]
Midfield Skill [ ]
Attack Skill [ ]

Opponents
[ ] Attack Skill
[ ] Midfield Skill
[ ] Defence Skill

Add 1 to each of your Skill totals if you're playing a home game, otherwise subtract 1. You may split your Morale and Fitness among your Skill scores however you wish.

Referee's Watch | 15 | 30 | 45 | 60 | 75 | 90 |

Substitutes & Scorers

....
....
....
....

Fact Sheet

Budget: £ [   ] **million**

Fixture List

Group Stage

Date	Home Team	Result	Away Team
Wednesday 15th	Hardwick City		Revolyutsiya Apelsyn
Tuesday 21st	Bayern Badetuch		Hardwick City
Wednesday 29th	Hardwick City		Kött Fotbollar

Quarters

Date	Home Team	Result	Away Team
Tuesday 4th			
Friday 7th			

Semis

Date	Home Team	Result	Away Team
Tuesday 11th			
Friday 14th			

Final

Date	Home Team	Result	Away Team
Saturday 22nd			

Morale: [   ]

Fitness: [   ]

Clues and Equipment:

Management Information:

Manager Qualities:

Additional Staff:

Squad Details

Player Name	Position	Skill	Injuries, cards, special skills
Jamie Coates	Goalkeeper	5	
Rob Rose	Goalkeeper	5	
	Goalkeeper		
Steve Fitzgerald	Defender	5	
Barry Voss	Defender	5	
Antek Bobak	Defender	5	
Howie Jevons	Defender	5	
Carlos de Carvalho	Defender	6	
	Defender		
	Defender		
Will Frost	Midfielder	5	
Zoki Roberts	Midfielder	6	
Anthony Bostock	Midfielder	5	
Klaus Wehnert	Midfielder	6	
John Hoggart	Midfielder	5	
Dmitri Duval	Midfielder	6	
	Midfielder		
	Midfielder		
Ben Parker	Attacker	6	
Salvatore Duce	Attacker	5	
Ian Leslie	Attacker	5	
Jed Stevens	Attacker	5	
Danny Knox	Attacker	7	
	Attacker		
	Attacker		

Remember, if a player is sent off, he must miss the next match as well.

Acknowledgements

The people to whom I'm indebted are too numerous to mention, being the whole of the sporting world on television, radio and the internet. TV commentary, Five Live phone-ins and post-match interviews have all been invaluable. I would like to thank Jonathan Pearce for making truth stranger than any fiction. John Motson and Clive Tyldesley have taught me a whole new language. Graeme Souness, Stuart Pearce, Gary Megson, Paul Gascoigne, Barry Davis and Derek Johnstone have all hit the back of the net more than once. But the unlikely golden goose this time has been the redoubtable Justin Langer, for inspiration beyond my wildest imaginings. You beauty!

www.bigmatchmanager.com

www.bloomsbury.com